COMING HOME TO LOVE

ECHO RIDGE ROMANCE #4

RACHELLE J. CHRISTENSEN

Praise for

Rachelle J. Christensen's
Echo Ridge Romance Series

Hope for Christmas

"This sweet romance is the perfect holiday read and will make you believe in the power of love and happily ever after."

—Cindy Roland Anderson, author of *Under a Georgia Moon*

The Kiss Thief

"Don't miss this romantic escape to the beautiful Echo Ridge with one of my favorite clean and fast-paced romance authors, Rachelle Christensen."

--Cami Checketts, author of *Don't Date Your Brother's Best Friend*

The Princess Bride of Riodan

"I disappeared into this book and the sweet town of Echo Ridge for the evening. Can't wait to go back!"

—Lucy McConnell, author of the *Dating Mr. Baseball* series

Coming Home to Love

"Rachelle Christensen creates a town we'd all like to live in and people we'd all like to be friends with."

—Janette Rallison, author of *How I Met Your Brother*

Diamond Rings Are Deadly Things (Wedding Planner Mysteries #1)

Veils and Vengeance (#2)

Proposals and Poison (#3)

The Soldier's Bride (A Music Box Romance #1)

Carve Me a Melody (A Music Box Romance #2)

Hawaiian Masquerade (Burke Billionaire Romance #1)

The Billionaire's Stray Heart (Burke Billionaire Romance #2)

The Refugee's Billionaire (Burke Billionaire Romance #3)

How to Fetch a Fiancé

River Whispers

Hope for Christmas: An Echo Ridge Romance #1

The Kiss Thief: An Echo Ridge Romance #2

The Princess Bride of Riodan: An Echo Ridge Romance #3

Coming Home to Love: An Echo Ridge Romance #4

Her Guy Next Door Fake Fiancé: Echo Ridge Romance #5

Novellas:

Silver Cascade Secrets

Double Take

Claire's Christmas Dance

ISBN: 978-1-949319-12-5

Coming Home to Love

Original Cover Design: Steven Novak

Cover Design © Peachwood Press

Published by Peachwood Press, May 2018

❀ Created with Vellum

Get your free book!

Dear Reader,

I'm delighted you've come back to visit the town of Echo Ridge, New York! If this is your first visit, I'm glad to have you! Each book in the Echo Ridge Romance series can be read as a stand-alone.

In this fourth book of the series, you'll discover the story of Billy Redford, the handsome carpenter you might have met in *The Princess Bride of Riodan.* Readers loved Billy's character and wanted to know more about his story. You'll also meet Laney Richins, a native of Echo Ridge coming back home.

Thank you for investing your time to read my book. I am so grateful for your support! You are the reason I write. If you enjoy this book, please consider leaving a review at your favorite online store. Each and every one helps me as an author.

Thank you and happy reading!

Rachelle

*L*aney Richins adjusted the cellophane around a dozen pink roses and inhaled the sweet scent. If only her life could be as uncomplicated and beautiful as roses. She pulled a crumpled petal away from one of the buds, her fingers lingering on the velvety texture. There was so much that Laney regretted, but like the rose, there was much more to her than the crumpled petals on the outside. With a shake of her head, Laney dismissed that train of thought and adjusted the silver ribbon.

She and her five-year-old son Oliver were happy in their little two-bedroom apartment. Happy to be far away from her ex-husband and just down the street from Grandpa and Grandma Richins. Laney didn't even mind the brunt of the summertime heat and humidity as August descended on Echo Ridge, New York. After eight years away, Laney had returned to her hometown—the same place she'd spurned and claimed she'd never come back to. She crouched down to snip a few wilted leaves from a fern and ended up sweeping up several of the tiny leaves from a low shelf. She had her head underneath the fronds of the fern when she heard the back door open. Maybe Paisley had forgotten something. Laney smiled, waiting for her sometimes-scatterbrained boss to call out.

"Laney?"

The person calling her name was definitely not Paisley Scott. It was a man, and she would know that voice anywhere, although it had matured to a more sultry tone. Even the note of surprise in the voice was recognizable. She turned slowly toward Billy Redford. His dark blond hair was cut short along the sides with a bit of a wave on top. He stood a head taller than her, at nearly six feet, and his skin was bronzed by the late summer sun. He was the same Billy from her high school days, but even better looking than her memories. His blue eyes widened, as if he hadn't believed it could really be her.

"Billy? What are you doing here?" She stood and brushed stray leaves from her knees, clenching her clippers tight enough in one hand that the handles bit into her skin.

"I came by to take some measurements for the new shelves Paisley needs."

Laney's heart pounded in her chest and her cheeks warmed at the sight of his broad shoulders and the scruff along his jawline. She couldn't figure out why he was measuring shelves for Paisley. The last she'd heard, Billy had graduated from college in construction management. "No, I meant, what are you doing here—as in Echo Ridge."

Billy arched an eyebrow. "I live here."

Laney's mouth dropped open. "Since when?"

"Almost a year ago." He tilted his head. "What are you doing here?"

"I moved back two weeks ago."

"No, I meant what are you doing here—as in Paisley's Petals."

Laney couldn't help but smile. Billy was teasing her just like old times—but no, that wasn't right. There was a look in his eyes that wasn't familiar. The way his jaw tightened as if he were biting back words made Laney take a step back. "I work here."

"Is this some kind of prank?" He turned and looked behind him. "I mean, you don't really want to live and work in Echo Ridge, do you?"

The words struck Laney like a bucket of water. They were words similar to those she'd thrown at Billy several times during their senior year. And then, that summer after graduation, she'd stomped on his dreams of staying in the small town to raise a family. She claimed that nothing could keep her in Echo Ridge and anyone who wanted to live and work there was small-minded.

She pulled her foot along the faded linoleum. "I deserve that I guess, but it's true nonetheless. I'm back in Echo Ridge to stay *and* I work here." Laney had never wanted to come back to Echo Ridge—the place where she was supposed to marry her high school sweetheart and raise her children. She'd turned her back on all of them, running after Dane and his sugar-sweet promises. She had Oliver and there was no regret there, but she wished she could undo other parts of her past.

Billy opened his mouth at the same time Paisley breezed into the shop. "Oh, hello, Billy. I'm glad you were able to make it in." She flipped her long brown braid over her shoulder and smiled. "I see you've met Laney. She and I were just talking earlier about how nice it will be to have some storage space. It's really nice of you to take this on. I know it's not what Redbuilt usually does."

Laney nodded, wondering if Paisley could pick up on the tension emanating between them. If she did, she chose to ignore it. She took Billy's arm and steered him toward the back wall while talking over her shoulder to include Laney. "Carlos has helped me in the past, but he's swamped and was kind enough to mention you."

"I don't mind," Billy answered. "We just poured the foundation for a new home by Ruby Mountain so my crew can handle things for a few days."

"Wait, who is Redbuilt?" Laney asked.

"It's my company," Billy answered. "Located *here* in Echo Ridge." His words had an edge to them and Laney caught the underlying jab again.

"That's marvelous. This town needs good construction companies. My parents mentioned how much it's growing, but I didn't believe them until I came home." She winked and was rewarded with a look of surprise from Billy. The bell over the front entrance rang, indicating a customer. "I'll help out front," Laney said. She walked away, knowing that just like old times, she'd been able to throw Billy for a loop. She had a genuine smile when she reached the customer.

Twenty minutes later, Laney finished an impromptu arrangement that Mrs. Tumnus needed for the library board meeting. The flowers were to celebrate Jennifer Staples finishing her degree in library science. Laney had seen her working in the young adult section of the library last time she went in. Once the silver-haired lady had exited the shop, Laney headed to the back to see what help she could offer Paisley. Her stomach clenched as she approached the area where Billy had been working, but her nerves unwound when she discovered he wasn't there.

"Looking for Billy?" Paisley poked her head around the corner. "He took some measurements and he won't be back until tomorrow night. Strange thing, that. Originally he'd planned to work all day tomorrow to get the project done, but suddenly he was too busy to be here during regular hours." Paisley arched an eyebrow in Laney's direction.

Laney shrugged. "That's probably for the best don't you think? Then we won't be tripping over each other."

Paisley snipped the end of a red rose and handed it to Laney. "They say every rose has a story and when it's given in love, the story is about the person who receives it."

"Hmm, I hadn't heard that before," Laney replied. "But you're the expert when it comes to flowers."

Paisley nodded and handed another rose to Laney. "True, you've only been here a couple weeks, but you have a gift with flower arranging, if you'll let yourself see it."

Laney looked down at the two roses, their buds barely beginning to open and spiral outward with velvet petals reaching toward the light. She lifted them to her nose and inhaled. "Thank you."

Paisley handed her three more roses. "If you'll add those to the Hyatt's funeral arrangement, I'll help you finish up."

Laney nodded and walked over to the refrigerated

unit that held several arrangements for the funeral. Winston Hyatt had been her seventh-grade science teacher and although he was in his late eighties, it was still hard to come to terms with the fact that people Laney had grown up around were dying. Those precious years of her childhood held magic, memories, and so much discovery. Every person in Echo Ridge had played a part in raising Laney Richins.

Even though she tried to convince herself it wasn't true, she couldn't help thinking that the best years of her life had been wasted and she wouldn't get a second chance to make the right choice. She didn't want to waste the chance this town was willing to give her. Everyone in Echo Ridge had opened their arms to the Laney they remembered, even if she was no longer that girl—everyone except Billy.

CHAPTER 2

*B*illy pushed his foot down on the gas pedal as he sped away from the center of Echo Ridge. He would rather have walked through a hornet's nest than discover that he would be working next to Laney Richins. High school was eight years in his past, but when he'd walked into Paisley's Petals and nearly tripped over his high school sweetheart, his heart had jumped back in time. For a second, when he'd looked into her chocolate-brown eyes, he'd almost forgotten how Laney had broken his heart, and every promise she'd made. He growled and gripped the steering wheel. They were teenagers back then, he knew that. Promises between two kids didn't mean anything, but time hadn't softened the blow that Laney had dealt him when she'd scorned her hometown, him, and his dreams.

It was ridiculous to feel this way, but Billy was

already trying to find a way to keep from running into Laney again. Why hadn't anyone told him that she'd come back to town? Of course, if it had been only two weeks, she might have been keeping a low-profile. Billy found himself turning down Aspen drive towards his parents' home. Last week at Sunday dinner, his sister, Kelli had started to mention something about a new family in town and his mother had shut her down. Billy had a strange feeling that maybe his family had known about Laney's arrival. The thought was enough to propel him forward. He parked his truck in the driveway and dashed up to the front door, knocking once and entering.

"Mom, are you home?"

"In the kitchen," she answered.

Billy rounded the corner and saw his mother, Norma Redford, working a large mound of dough. "Hi, Mom." He kissed her cheek, catching a whiff of the floral perfume she always wore.

"Hi yourself." She pinched off a glob of dough, shaped it into a ball and placed it on a greased baking sheet. She had a smear of flour on her cheek that matched the gray sprinkled throughout her dark blond hair. "I'm making rolls for Winston Hyatt's funeral tomorrow."

"I'll sit next to you and Dad. Mr. Hyatt was my favorite seventh-grade teacher." Billy snagged a piece of dough and popped it into his mouth. "I'll be sure to stop by later and taste-test them if you need."

Norma pointed to the mound of dough. "If you're here for a minute, you might as well help. That'd be better than snitching all my dough and getting a belly-ache." Norma's blue eyes sparkled, and Billy was reminded how often Laney had commented that he'd inherited his mother's eyes. He shook his head. He needed to stop thinking about Laney.

"How is Mrs. Hyatt doing?"

"Evangeline is taking his passing well, but she's putting their property up for sale. Too much work for a woman her age."

"Wow, that's moving rather fast for Mrs. Hyatt, isn't it?" Billy washed his hands in the sink and joined his mother in shaping rolls.

"Well, Winston's health was failing for the past three years and they had already decided to move to the senior community. I hope she'll be able to sell it. That place needs a lot of work, especially the old barn."

Billy remembered how much he'd loved the Hyatts' property as a kid. It was a couple miles outside of Echo Ridge and with the pasture, barn, and woodworking shop, it felt like it was in a country all by itself. "Laney and I used to sneak out there and throw rocks up in the rafters of the barn to spook the bats. They'd swoop out and Laney would scream with that high-pitched shriek.

I was always sure she was going to wake the neighbors." He swallowed, trying to phrase the next question casually. "Did you know she was back in town?"

"I heard." Norma kept her head down, pinching dough and smoothing it into balls.

Billy squeezed the dough so tight, it squished between his fingers. "You knew? Why didn't you say something?" Billy leaned down to look at his mother. "I ran into her at Paisley's today and I don't even know what came out of my mouth. I still can't believe that she's really here."

"I hope you weren't unkind to her."

Billy groaned. "Mom, you should have told me she was here. I'm a big boy now. Besides, Laney is married. She probably has a family. I'm not interested in her."

Norma clucked her tongue. "Laney is divorced, and it was a tough situation. She has a little boy. I think he's four or five. She came home because she needs help."

"She's divorced?" For some reason, his heart lurched in his chest. Laney had married and divorced and he had yet to find the right woman, even though he'd been pretty close a couple years ago. "How do you know all this?"

"I saw Josi at the library a couple days after Laney moved back. She told me that Laney was worried about how people would react to her return. I think she really needs a friend."

Laney's mother, Josi Richins, was like a second mother to him. Billy hadn't reconnected with her like he should have since moving back to Echo Ridge. At the time he'd been nursing his own wounded heart when his girlfriend of two years had decided to move to California with no strings attached. He shook his head, trying to dislodge the guilt and the memories. "Laney's not here to stay. She'll take what she needs and then leave."

Norma brushed her hands on her apron. "Billy, that's no way to speak about a woman you loved."

"She was a girl. I was a boy. We've both grown up."

"Maybe you haven't grown up as much as you think." Norma pinched his side. "You could still use more meat on these bones."

"I'd better get back to work." Billy jumped on the change of subject and washed his hands again. "Thanks for letting me stop by."

"Thanks for helping me with the rolls. I'll see you tomorrow."

Billy pulled out of the driveway and headed toward the Hyatts' farm. He drove until he caught sight of the realtor's sign hanging next to the white-fenced property. Billy pulled up beside it and gazed at the familiar structures. Some parts of the barn were over one hundred years old. The wood shop was the original homestead, and nearly two-hundred years old. The Hyatt's brick home was newer, but still a hundred years if it was a day. His mother was right. Everything needed a lot of work. Billy jotted down the number. He told himself that he was just curious, but deep down, he knew it was more than that. He'd always dreamed of raising a family on a farm like the Hyatts'. Working in the shop, fixing up the barn, raising chickens, and riding horses—it was a dream that he'd shared with Laney when they were young. She had loved the idea and told him that she would be a city mouse and a country mouse at the same time if she could live like the Hyatts.

It seemed like every good memory he had growing up was touched by Laney Richins. They weren't just high school sweethearts, they were best friends. When she left, she took a piece of his heart with her. Up until the moment he saw her today, he hadn't realized it, but all these years later, Billy worried that maybe Laney still had that piece of his heart.

Billy waited until six o'clock that evening before returning to Paisley's Petals with the building materials for the new shelving. Paisley had given him a key and he breathed a sigh of relief when he turned the doorknob and found it locked, indicating that Laney was gone. He unlocked the door and began unloading his equipment.

Space was at a premium inside the relic of a building so the shelves would be a welcome addition to the flower shop. Billy whistled as he cleared the space of a roll of cellophane, green foam squares, and some miscellaneous pots. With a thick pencil, he measured and marked on the wall where he planned to mount the first shelf. The job was an easy one—it didn't require much skill, but Billy was thankful that people around Echo Ridge were starting to recognize Redbuilt Construction as a viable company.

After college, he'd worked with a large construction firm and enjoyed a nice salary with benefits. He could've stayed at that job and eventually been a site manager, but Billy was willing to do odd jobs to build up his own company so that he could manage his life and work towards finding the kind of success that he valued. Aside from Paisley's shelves, he was remodeling a walk-in closet for Kirke and Jennifer Staples and building a special bookstack for the new children's book section in the basement of the Echo Ridge library. Billy whistled a happy tune when he recalled how excited Britta Klein and Marian Montgomery were when he started the long-awaited project. Billy knelt down and screwed in the bottom shelf. Every time he thought about the house plans for Chelsea and Drew Stirling he felt a thrill that could only be compared to the way he'd felt when his dad bought him his first tool set at age six. He was lost in a memory when he heard Laney's voice.

"Hello, is someone here?"

Billy jerked back and banged his head on the shelf he'd just installed. "Ow!"

"Oh, dear." Laney came around the corner. "Billy, is that you?"

He sat up, rubbed the top of his head, and looked at the last person he wanted to see. Laney stood there gripping her keys, a worried expression on her face. She looked different than high school, but so much was the same. She had a few more curves, but the same tiny waist. Her dark brown hair was pulled up in a ponytail showing the curve of her neck where Billy used to love to plant kisses. Billy shook his head and motioned to the pile of boards and tools. "Yeah, I'm just banging around back here, don't mind me."

"Sorry to interrupt. I forgot to put this arrangement in the cooler. It's for Winston's funeral tomorrow." She walked over to a table with at least a dozen different potted plants and picked up one that was dotted with beautiful white roses and a large white bow. She slid back the glass door of the cooler and set the arrangement inside. "It's hard to believe that our teachers are dying. We're not that old."

"We aren't that old, but Mr. Hyatt was old when we were in seventh grade. I think most of our teachers will be around for a while yet." Billy watched her move with the grace that she'd always naturally carried. Laney was a little thing, not quite five-foot-three. Billy knew this because he loved to tease that he was ten inches taller than her which made him ten times more amazing. A smile tugged at the corners of his mouth and he refocused to find Laney studying him, her brown eyes sparkling with a hidden laugh.

"Lost you there for a minute, Red." Laney grinned, the dimple in her left cheek deepening.

She'd called him by his nickname and Billy's stomach tightened at the easy way she spoke, as if she hadn't been gone for years—as if she'd forgotten how she'd left him and their dreams for the future behind.

"Too much on my mind. I need to get these shelves done. Good luck with the flowers." He turned back toward the wall and lifted another shelf into place. Maybe if he ignored Laney she would go away.

"I'm glad you could work on them today. I was worried that I scared you off earlier and Paisley is so excited about these shelves."

"Yep." Billy clenched his jaw. Apparently ignoring Laney wasn't going to work. It had never worked when they were younger either. She had a tenacity that couldn't be discounted and she'd taught Billy a lot about the power of sticking to something.

"Well, I'm done here. Maybe I'll see you at the funeral

tomorrow." Laney paused next to Billy, close enough that he didn't dare turn around.

"Have a good night," he muttered.

"Thanks, you too."

Once the door clicked shut, Billy groaned and rubbed a hand over his face. Memories of his past were battling with the present and trying to derail the future that he'd carefully planned. He would not let Laney mess with his head or his heart again.

CHAPTER 3

*L*aney turned the radio up and sang along with a country song, focusing on each word so that she wouldn't think about Billy Redford. She drove across town to the cul de sac where her parents still lived. Oliver was there playing in their back yard. Her cute five year old would be starting kindergarten next week at Echo Ridge Elementary. They'd hardly spent any time apart while Laney was a stay-at-home mom. After her divorce last year, she'd worked odd jobs from home and at daycares so that she could care for Oliver. The job at Paisley's Petals was the first full-time position she'd held since before Oliver was born.

Her parents loved having Oliver nearby and they'd agreed to watch him while Laney ran to the flower shop to rescue the white rose arrangement. She'd been surprised to see Billy there and for a moment she felt like they'd stepped back in time when they were best friends and they joked, laughed, teased, and loved every minute they spent together.

But right about the moment she'd called him Red, Billy had turned ice-cold and not made eye contact again. It didn't matter. Laney had memorized every feature of the boy she once loved. She could see Billy's crystal blue eyes and the way his dark blond hair curled over his ears, but the broad shoulders with muscles corded along his back—that was new. Billy wasn't a boy anymore, he was a man. She'd tried not to notice the way his t-shirt was snug against his biceps—okay, she hadn't tried at all. She'd ogled Billy and all his muscles down to the carpenter's pants that fit just right with the assortment of tools hanging from his tool belt. But it was only because she hadn't seen him for so long, right?

Laney shrugged and pulled up to her parent's house. By the time she walked around the house to the back-yard where Oliver was squealing and giggling, she'd forgotten all about Billy Redford—at least that's what she told herself.

Laney wasn't surprised to see more than half the town of Echo Ridge turn out for Winston Hyatt's funeral. Laney and Paisley set up all the flowers before nine that morning and the funeral hall looked beautiful. The evidence of so much love and appreciation for Winston warmed Laney's heart. Echo Ridge was a good place with good people. It still didn't feel quite like the home she'd left, but Laney figured that was because she wasn't the same girl who had left that home. She caught sight of Oliver, dressed in his little gray suit and tugging at his tie with a frown. Laney ducked her head to hide a smile. She was a mother now, and Oliver had changed her for the better, bringing small joys to everyday life.

When she lifted her head again, she caught sight of Billy sitting next to his parents. Lee and Norma looked great and as Laney watched, Norma caught her eye and smiled brightly. Norma nudged Billy who looked up and met her eye, but he didn't smile. He turned to his mother, whispered something and put his head back down. Laney felt her face heat up, and she quickly turned and walked in the other direction, taking the long route back to her seat beside Oliver.

The funeral service was peaceful with lovely music and an interesting life sketch, but Laney's mind kept wandering back to Billy. It didn't seem that long ago that she could make him laugh with one arch of her eyebrow, but he'd met her gaze and not even cracked a smile. When she had married Dane, Laney had ignored the whispers from her parents about Billy's broken heart, thinking that it couldn't be true. They were kids who didn't really know anything about love. But sitting in the funeral hall today, Laney had to admit that she'd learned a lot about love in the past few years. The truth was that she'd broken both of their hearts and they'd mended into something misshapen, something that was never meant to be.

Would she and Billy ever be friends again? It was better not to dwell on that thought. It hurt too much. She concentrated on helping Paisley move some of the arrangements to the luncheon hall. The red roses Laney had clipped for the arrangement still looked fresh and beautiful. Laney adjusted the greenery and when she looked up, she gasped. Oliver was a few steps in front of her and he was just reaching up his hand to pull on Billy's hand. Billy was talking to his mother and Elise's grandmother, Suzy Gibson. There was an easy smile on his face. Laney gripped the flower arrangement and for a half-second thought about sprinting to Oliver or at least calling out to him to stop, but her feet were glued to the carpet. All she could do was watch as his tiny fingers reached out to Billy's large hand.

"Hey, you're in my grandma's house. I saw you," Oliver said as he tugged on Billy's hand.

Billy turned and smiled down at the Oliver. "Well, hello there. What's your name?"

Don't tell him, Laney wanted to say. *Just walk away*, but of course her little chatterbox kept up his end of the conversation. Should she hide behind the flower arrangement or say hello?

"I'm Oliver." He cocked his head to one side. "How did you get in my grandma's house?"

Billy's brow furrowed and he chuckled, glancing at Josi and Suzy. "Hmm, let me see. Who is your grandma?"

Oliver pointed at Josi Richins. "That's my grandma. Don't you know?"

Josi laughed. "Oliver, you are a hoot."

Billy looked up and his eyes met Laney's. He stiffened, glanced at Oliver, and then back at her. It was enough to jolt her into movement and she smiled clutching the arrangement tighter. "Oliver, are you minding your manners?"

"Mommy, mommy! This is the guy in grandma's pictures and he was holding you." Oliver pointed at Billy.

Laney cringed, her mother had never removed the shrine to her only daughter's high school years in the guest bedroom. The picture that Oliver had recognized was one of Josi's favorites. Billy had been holding her in his arms and they'd both been smiling at the camera for their senior year homecoming dance. Laney had asked her mother to get rid of that photo at least a dozen times, but she'd never have dreamed that her son would recognize Billy from the photo.

Billy wiped a hand over his face, the tips of his ears

turning pink. Josi came to his rescue. "Billy, I'm glad you could meet Oliver. He's quite precocious, just like his mother."

"I'm glad to meet you, Oliver." Billy took Oliver's hand and shook it gently.

"So you know my mom," Oliver asked.

Laney stepped forward and took Oliver's hand. "Yes, we went to school together." Laney hesitated, how could she explain their relationship? Billy beat her to it.

"We were good friends," Billy answered. "It was nice talking with you, Josi. Take care of yourself Suzy." Billy smiled and walked toward the open doors at the end of the hall.

That hurt was back again, even though Billy's exit had appeared gracious and timely. Josi arched an eyebrow in Laney's direction, but Laney just pressed her lips together and tugged on Oliver's hand. "Come help Mommy with a few of these plants."

"Okay." Oliver smiled and skipped along beside her, unaware of what he'd just put in motion.

After the services were over and the last relative had taken the potted ivy, Laney took Oliver's hand and exited the building.

"Mommy, can I take off my tie now?" Oliver tugged at the tie and it started to unzip.

"Yes, sweetie. Let me help you." Laney unzipped the tie and slipped it off his neck.

"Ah, that's better." Oliver smiled and Laney chuckled.

"Let's go get changed and I'll drop you off at Grandma's house."

Oliver grinned. "I love Grandma and Grandpa's house!"

"Me, too." Laney ruffled his hair and helped him into the car.

There was still plenty of work to do at the flower shop and Laney found herself looking forward to it, wondering if she'd catch sight of Billy again. She shook her head and forced Billy from her mind.

CHAPTER 4

Friday afternoon, Billy was driving across town to get started on the framing of Drew and Chelsea's house when his sister called.

"Hey, Billy. Do you have a minute?" Kelli asked.

"That depends on what you want."

"Why do you think I want something?" Kelli's voice pitched higher.

Billy smiled. His sister worked as a counselor at Echo Ridge High and since moving back, she'd roped Billy into more than one school project. "Because you only call me during the day when you need something."

Kelli groaned. "I wanted to wait until tonight, but I have plans with Greg. He's taking me on an actual date."

"Well, I hope you have fun. I'm almost to my job site. Do you want me to save you some time and just say no right now?"

"Billy!"

He chuckled. "What?"

"Listen, I'm over the Homecoming committee this year at the school and we just had our planning meeting. The theme is Sailing the High Seas and we have all kinds of great things planned for homecoming week."

"That sounds great. I bet it'll be a success with you heading it up."

"Praise won't do you any good. I have a favor to ask you and I want you to say yes."

He coughed. "I think I'm coming down with something. Maybe I'd better hang up before I lose my voice."

Kelli snorted and continued as if she hadn't heard him. "We want to have a unique backdrop for the photos that will act as the main decoration for the dance too. A pirate ship, a bridge, something to do with pirates. They asked if there were any carpenters around that might be willing to help the school."

"Kelli, I'm really busy right now. I hope you didn't volunteer me for this." Billy had already spent the better part of a Saturday helping out on The Santorini Café's float. Wyatt Nelson and Garrett Halifax had lured half the town into helping build the float that Wyatt's sister had designed.

"I didn't volunteer you. I'm asking you right now if you'll help us out. It won't be hard and you'll have help. Everyone on the committee is busy calling people right now to get the help we need for all the preparations."

Billy coughed again. "I think I might be contagious. Are you sure you want me to contaminate the school?"

"I'll take the risk," Kelli said. "So can you help me?"

"You want me to build some kind of setup that has to do with pirates for the backdrop?"

"Yes. The dance is Saturday, the twenty-sixth."

"Wait. It's in August? I thought homecoming was always in September?"

"It moves around every year to accommodate some of the sports tournaments. But this year, it's one week earlier than usual," Kelli explained. "That's why we're in a bind. We're barely starting school and having to plan homecoming."

Billy remembered being on the homecoming committee when he was a senior in high school. He'd helped build the photo backdrop and Laney had decorated it to look like a fifties diner. He still had the picture somewhere.

"So, is that a yes or did you hang up on me?" Kelli interrupted his thoughts.

Billy groaned. "I don't know when I'm supposed to have time to work on it, but yes, because you're my favorite sister, I'll help you."

"I'm your only sister," Kelli replied. "Thanks, Billy. I know you'll come up with something great. I'll give your number to the committee and they'll call you with more info, but I'll keep tabs on you too."

"Okay, but you owe me big time."

"Double chocolate oatmeal cookies?"

Billy's stomach stood at attention. "Two dozen."

"Done."

"I'd like one dozen as a down payment and the second dozen can be delivered upon completion."

Kelli laughed. "You got it, bro."

After Billy ended the call, he smiled. Kelli did call in a lot of favors but she was a great sister and Billy loved her two kids, Bronson and Miley. Her husband Greg was easy to get along with too. Billy enjoyed spending time with his family. It was one of the reasons he'd decided to come back home to Echo Ridge to start his business.

When he pulled up to the job site, he took a few minutes to sketch out some ideas for the photo backdrop. He could build most of it using lumber scraps and his business could donate a few sheets of plywood. After the dance, he could salvage some of the lumber back to recoup his costs. He nodded his head. Maybe helping Kelli out wouldn't be so bad after all.

Laney pulled some wilted leaves off a houseplant and spritzed the shelf full of potted plants. She glanced at the new shelving that Billy had finished last night. Apparently he'd snuck in after hours to complete the job because Laney hadn't seen him even though she'd lingered for an extra half-hour tidying up after the shop closed. Paisley had already filled up half the shelves, rearranging their storage room and opening up a new workspace.

"Hi, Aunt Laney," Alex said.

She turned around to see her nephew standing next to a bunch of red roses.

"Alex, you grow taller every time I see you. You remind me so much of Cody when we were kids." Laney gave him a side-armed hug. It was still hard to believe that her older brother had a teenage son and two daughters. She felt like she was behind the game, divorced and with only one little boy who had been remarkable through life's recent upheaval.

"What brings you here?"

Alex licked his lips. "Well, I'm on the homecoming committee at school."

"You are!" Laney clapped her hands. "I love homecoming! I was on the committee my senior year. We decorated like the fifties. It was so fun."

"I was thinking that it might be your kind of thing, so I wondered if you could help me out?"

"Of course," Laney said. "What do you need me to do?"

"Well, we want to have a fancy backdrop for the photos that can also be used as a decoration for the dance theme. It's Sailing the High Seas and we'd like it to feature pirates," Alex said. "Can you be in charge of decorating it?"

"Wow, that sounds like a big job. So you'd be helping me, right?"

Alex nodded. "Yes, and we have a great committee. All the students and teachers were assigned to contact different people in Echo Ridge who might be willing to help."

"Well, as long as I can juggle this with my work, I think I can help," Laney said.

"Great!" Alex appeared relieved. "We're having another planning meeting Monday morning. Could you make it if we held it at nine?"

"Yes, I usually don't start here until ten, so that works great."

"Awesome. I told everyone that I have the best aunt."

Laney arched an eyebrow. "Well, a little praise never hurt anybody. I'll see you Monday, Alex."

After Alex left, Laney started humming as she worked. She'd finished up two orders before she realized that the song was the same one that she'd danced to under the disco ball at the homecoming dance with Billy

Redford. They had been crowned the homecoming King and Queen, and the night couldn't have been more perfect. It wasn't a surprise that they had won because everyone knew that Billy and Laney were meant to be.

Laney frowned. It wasn't long after that homecoming dance that she'd started to get restless. Echo Ridge had changed from the sleepy little town she loved into some sort of prison that she needed to escape. And she had escaped, but life outside her prison walls had been very different than what she'd imagined. Seeing Billy had brought back memories that she'd stuffed deep inside and now she felt an undeniable yearning to revisit those times. She had loved Billy, and later realized that she didn't fully understand love, but she did understand friendship. Billy had been her best friend and she missed him. She missed his easy smile and his deep chuckle. Laney pressed her lips together. She couldn't take back what she'd abandoned—Billy had indicated as much when he saw her at the funeral and he couldn't even smile in her direction. Still, there was a tiny part of her that wished for a chance to right the wrongs she'd committed.

CHAPTER 5

*L*aney went to work Saturday morning for a couple hours to finish up some silk arrangements. Paisley was letting Lacey Johnson, the new owner of The Santorini Café, use the arrangements for their float during the upcoming Homecoming parade. After work, Laney picked up Oliver and took him to story time at the Echo Ridge Library. On the way she kept looking for Billy's red truck, the one she'd seen a few times with his Redbuilt logo on the side. She still couldn't make sense of the few interactions they'd had—maybe the library would have a riveting novel she could read to take her mind off of Billy. She stepped into the old church, remodeled into a beautiful setting for book lovers, and took a deep breath. The scent of new and old books mixed together hinted of stories that couldn't be left alone. She led Oliver over to a display of new books.

He crouched down and scanned the bright covers of the beginning readers and Laney snatched up the latest book by Heather Tullis.

"Laney? Is that you?"

Laney turned to meet the clear blue eyes of Britta Klein. The head librarian of Echo Ridge had dated Laney's brother in high school, and she'd always been nice to Laney. "Britta! I heard you had taken over the library. It looks wonderful here. I bet you love it."

Britta hugged Laney. "It's so great to see you. I didn't believe it when Milo told me he thought you were back in town."

"Milo? Who's that?"

Britta smiled and her cheeks turned pink. "Milo Geissler is my fiancé. He's a piano tuner here in Echo Ridge."

"What!" Laney grabbed Britta's hand and pulled it forward examining the silver band with a square-cut diamond. "I'm so happy for you. When are you getting married?"

Britta's smile widened. "April fourteenth. I'm so excited!"

"Oh, a springtime wedding in Echo Ridge," Laney said. "Britta, that is wonderful news. I hope you'll send me an invite."

"Of course." Britta glanced at her ring. "You know how bossy your brother can be. Cody already told me that he was on the invite list because he's friends with Milo."

"I can practically hear him saying that." Laney chuckled. "I'm happy for you." She motioned to the arching stairway of the library, the white plaster had been repainted and it was a lovely contrast to the many colors contained in the stacks of books. "This was always your dream, wasn't it?"

Britta looked up toward the high ceilings of the library. "Yes. I love it here." She turned back to Laney. "Tell me how you've been. What have you been up to?"

"Well, you probably heard that I'm divorced. And this is my son, Oliver." Laney nodded to Oliver who sat at her feet, flipping through a picture book.

"He's adorable." Britta leaned close to Oliver. "How old are you?"

Oliver lifted his head and held up his hand with fingers outstretched. "I'm five. I'm going to kindergarten!"

"You're going to do great. I bet you're going to love reading in school."

Oliver nodded. "I like books."

Britta's face softened and she straightened. "I did hear about your divorce. I'm really sorry things didn't work out."

Laney shrugged and swallowed back the bitterness in her throat. "Things get better every day. I was lucky enough to get a job working at Paisley's Petals. I've always loved flowers, but I had no idea how much work went into running a flower shop. Paisley is amazing."

"I can see you working there with all of your energy. I bet she loves having you."

"Well, she was desperate," Laney said. "Elise Gibson left with hardly any notice to run off with that prince. Paisley was swamped trying to keep up with things."

"Oh, I remember that," Britta said. "Wasn't it around the same time the tabloids went crazy over Prince Titan?"

"Yeah, that was it," Laney said. "I thought that kind of stuff only happened in the movies, but Elise is living it."

"I met her prince. He seemed totally down to earth. If it weren't for all of the tabloids featuring Titan, I wouldn't have known it was him."

"I'm happy for Elise. She was always kind to everyone in high school."

"You had a good group of kids to run with," Britta said. "I don't have as many fond memories from high school as you, but now that I've found my place here it doesn't bother me."

"I'm glad to hear that," Laney said. "I haven't had time to stop in here since I got back. Oliver was so excited to come for story time today."

"That doesn't start for another thirty minutes," Britta

said. "That means you'll have enough time for a tour of the new children's section."

"A tour, huh?" Laney held out her hand, indicating the one room library.

"It's downstairs. The entire space has been renovated."

"Really?" Laney looked toward the old elevator that had always been off limits to library patrons. That hadn't stopped Billy from taking her for a ride one night in the rickety contraption. Laney was scared of heights and she'd clung to him like a kitten. He hadn't minded one bit.

Britta's alto voice pulled her from the memory. "We had a huge fundraiser last year. Everyone pitched in and even though the project took longer than we hoped, it's almost finished."

"A lot has happened in the last few years," Laney replied. "Sometimes I think if I'd been gone longer I might not have recognized this town when I returned."

"Change has a way of sneaking up on us, I guess."

Britta led the way down the stairs. Laney followed, helping Oliver down the wide staircase. The walls were painted light gray and yellow, and Laney noticed the beginning sketches for a mural across the largest wall. "Who will be painting that?"

"Do you remember Fay Griffith, well, Fay Sparks now?"

"Yeah, she runs the café just across the street, right?" Laney had stopped by for lunch last week. She and Oliver had enjoyed sandwiches and the softest chocolate chip cookies with chunks of chocolate melting in her mouth. Fay was a few years older than her, and Laney remembered her as being the artistic type in high school. Fay sported pink and purple streaks in her hair, and when she bustled around the café, Laney remembered thinking that Fay looked like she was happy.

"Yes, we begged her to help with this project. It doesn't pay the best, but Fay wanted to give back to the town." Britta stood in front of the wall and motioned to the lines waiting to be painted in. "We're lucky to have her talent."

Laney studied the drawing. It looked like rough sketches of trees with books hanging from the branches. She could only imagine the magic that Fay would bring out of the plain gray wall. "You're right. This is going to be fantastic."

"We have another artist, Jojo Halifax, who will be doing the mural on the other side of the basement."

"Wow, you weren't kidding when you said this is a huge project."

Britta grinned. "The grand re-opening of the library is going to be quite the event."

"Be sure to let us know."

"Mommy, can I look at those books?" Oliver tugged

on Laney's hands and pointed to a white bookshelf with a bench in front of it.

"Sure, Sweetie. Just stay where Mommy can see you."

"Billy is here somewhere. He's been in charge of the remodel. He installed the stacks for our children's books and came by for the final inspection before we start filling them with books." Britta turned toward the new bookshelves. "I should probably go check with him before he leaves."

"Oh, I bet he did a great job." Laney's heart tap-danced in her chest at the mention of Billy. She took a calming breath and told herself not to look for him, but her body didn't listen. She followed Britta toward the last of the large bookshelves stacked in a row of five across the basement.

Billy came around the end of the stack and smiled at Britta. "Looks like these are ready for books."

"Now we just need to get enough books to fill them all," Britta replied.

Billy wore carpenter jeans and the same toolbelt heavy with an assortment of tools. His light blue t-shirt reminded her of the clear blue color of his eyes. He looked good, even with a sheen of sweat on his fore-head. She took another step closer.

Billy motioned to the bookshelves. "I hope you—oh, hi Laney." He froze when he caught sight of her trailing behind Britta.

Laney lifted her hand in a wave. "Hi, Billy. Isn't this amazing? Britta was just showing me all that you've done for the children's section. You seem to be involved in everything around this town."

Billy started to smile, but then his face twitched and he pressed his lips together in a hard line. "It's been a lot of work." He turned to Britta. "I hope you don't mind, but I have to run to my next job. Everything will be ready to go here soon. Call me if you need anything."

Before Britta or Laney could answer, Billy turned and disappeared behind the stacks. Britta turned to Laney, a curious expression furrowing her brow. "What just happened?"

Laney pasted on a smile and shrugged. "Billy always was on the move. I think he's pretty busy. He just finished a project over at Paisley's shop."

Britta studied Laney, her brow relaxing. "Okay, well, it looks like it's almost story time. Shall we grab Oliver and go?"

Laney nodded and followed Britta toward her son who was immersed in a picture book about a giant strawberry. Did Billy really hate her so much that he couldn't even carry on a conversation? She didn't want to believe it but Laney worried that the man who was once her best friend had forgotten the very memories she'd been daydreaming about.

Monday morning Billy rushed from the job site of Drew and Chelsea's home to get to the planning meeting at the high school. Part of him was already wishing he hadn't agreed to help build the backdrop for the homecoming dance. Where was he going to come up with the extra hours he'd need to do that?

He pushed open the door and walked into the room. There were a couple high school students sitting at a table going over a checklist on a clipboard. He nodded when they looked up. "Sorry, I'm late. I hurried as fast as I could to get here."

"No problem," Kelli said, drawing his attention to the other side of the room. "Laney just got here too."

Billy jerked his head to the side and sure enough, there was Laney sitting next to her nephew, Alex

Richins. She smiled at him and he tried not to notice how good she looked in a dark pink shirt and with her brown hair pulled back in a low ponytail. He noticed anyway. And it bothered him. Why was she at the meeting? Billy swallowed hard and pulled up a chair next to Kelli. "Well, what do I need to know?"

Kelli handed him a typed page of notes, a mischievous glint in her eye. "You and Laney will be working together on the backdrop for the photos."

Laney sat up in her chair and coughed. She turned to Billy. "Oh. Well. Okay, then."

"Well, Laney can help with the decorating," Billy said. "I don't need any help with building."

Kelli tapped her clipboard with a pen. "You're building the framework and Laney is in charge of decorating it. We hoped that you two could work together."

Billy didn't look at Laney, but he could feel her staring at him. It reminded him of the game they used to play during high school. Laney would stare holes in the back of his head during a particularly boring history lecture until Billy sensed her attention. He would turn slowly and wink. She'd start laughing and end up in trouble, but because she was so darn cute she always seemed to find a way out of it.

"We're grateful that you can help us out," Kelli said to Billy. She smiled at Laney and her eyes twinkled.

"Mrs. Peterson, we're going to head down to the

office." Alex stood with the other high school students. "Roper said he'd finish making the copies of the fliers we're going to put up about the dance."

"Okay, thanks, Alex." Kelli turned to Billy. "Come take Alex's seat and we'll figure out what needs to happen next."

Billy arched an eyebrow at his sister. Her eyes danced with laughter as he sat in the seat Alex had just vacated. Next to Laney.

Laney didn't seem to mind, in fact, she scooted her chair closer to Billy. "I told Paisley what I was doing and she wants to help sponsor the backdrop. She has some great potted plants that might look nice against the setup."

"I thought the theme was pirates. Since when do pirates have plants on their ship?" Billy's voice was flat and he saw Laney stiffen at his tone.

"Since Laney already has an in for a sponsor." Kelli leaned forward, giving Billy a warning look. "There are plenty of options for decorating. Pirates often went to tropical islands to look for buried treasure. There's walking the plank. The pirate jail—what do they call that again?"

"The brig." both Billy and Laney answered simultaneously.

Laney grinned, but Billy looked away.

Kelli's phone buzzed and she grabbed it. "I have to take this call. Why don't you two talk for a few minutes and see what direction you'd like to go?"

Billy knew what direction he wanted to go—away. Far away from Laney Richins and her impetuous smile. And that dimple. The one he used to kiss to make Laney giggle. He closed his eyes and shook his head to clear the memories, but it didn't help. Erasing every memory of Laney would definitely help him forget his heartache but it would also erase his childhood.

"Billy?" Laney's voice was soft, filtering in through the slideshow of events that Billy wasn't willing to forget.

He opened his eyes and turned toward her voice.

She pressed her teeth against her bottom lip and sighed. "If you'd rather not work with me, I'm sure I can help out in some other way."

Her words slammed into his heart, and they shouldn't have hurt because he was over Laney Richins, wasn't he? But against his will, his hand reached out and touched Laney's and before he knew what was happening, his brain hijacked his tongue and he heard himself say, "I want to do this. I'm sorry I was acting grumpy. Kelli knows how busy I am, but she thinks because I don't have a family I have all the time in the world."

Laney smiled and squeezed Billy's hand. "I promise

we'll get it done in record time. Don't you remember the tree house we built?"

Billy snorted, pulling back his hand to cover his eyes. Of course he remembered the tree house they *attempted* to build. When they were nine years old. The two had scavenged broken wood planks, branches, pieces of tin and an old tarp and spent the afternoon working through an entire box of nails. When the masterpiece was finished, Laney had been the first one to step through the doorway which promptly collapsed. She got twelve stitches and a tetanus shot for their effort and Billy had to work for two weeks to earn enough money to buy his dad a box of nails. "Are you ever going to let me live that one down?"

Laney chuckled. "That was the best day, even though it didn't end how I hoped. It was the excitement and anticipation of building something on our own. We did that by ourselves, even if it wasn't up to code."

Billy shook his head. "Seeing you here sure does bring back a lot of memories."

"I feel the same way," Laney replied. "So, how about we build a brig where the students can stand inside and get their picture taken?"

"Only if you'll walk the plank," Billy said.

Laney straightened and held out her hand. "As long as someone's there to catch me, I'll walk the plank, Matey."

"Deal." Billy shook her hand, trying to ignore the slow burn creeping up his arm, igniting his heart. He was in trouble, but he was an expert at handling problems since he started his own company. He could handle this.

Laney leaned over the counter with a groan as soon as she returned from the meeting at the high school.

"That doesn't sound good," Paisley said.

Laney lifted her head. "They loved your idea, but I'm not sure I should be the one to help with the project after all."

"Why not? This is your hometown. It wasn't that long ago that you were going to the homecoming dance."

Laney remembered that night. It was the first time she'd voiced her concerns over living in such a small town. The first time she'd had any doubt about marrying Billy Redford. He'd been adamant about staying close to his roots and raising the kind of family they'd been lucky enough to be born into. After the dance, they'd had an argument over whether Echo Ridge was stifling or Laney was just being snobbish. Billy had accused her of trying to run away from who she really was, and Laney had been angry enough to refuse him a good night kiss. Later they'd made up and she'd pushed her doubts away for a few months. Everything had seemed fine between Billy and her until she'd realized that it wasn't.

Maybe it was a premonition of some sort and she'd ignored it, but the fact that she was back in Echo Ridge made her wonder if Billy had been right all along. Laney pulled herself from her memories and answered Paisley's question. "Somehow I was paired up with Billy Redford."

Paisley arched an eyebrow. "And why is that a bad thing? I thought you two were friends."

Laney splayed her fingers across the glass counter. "We were more than friends. We were high school sweethearts."

"And?"

"And I may have broken Billy's heart and told him I didn't want to live with him in Echo Ridge. He had our whole life planned out for us here, and I rejected him."

"Hmm." Paisley poked several stems of greenery into the foam core of an arrangement. "I don't see how that creates a problem now."

"You should have seen Billy. He didn't want anything to do with me."

"But he agreed to work with you in the end?" Paisley held up a rose and examined the petals, eying Laney over the top of the bud.

Laney picked up a broken stem and tossed it in the trash. "Yes, but he looked like he had a toothache."

"Well, next time you see him, give him the card for your dentist and pretend like you didn't notice his reluctance to work with you."

Laney laughed. "Paisley, you don't understand. I think Billy is uncomfortable being in the same room with me because we never really talked again after I . . ."

"Broke his heart?"

Laney tilted her head to the side. "Sometimes I wish I could go back in time, change my life, but still keep Oliver."

"You don't need to go back in time. You have a chance now to fix whatever is bothering you from your past. Don't let this opportunity go to waste." Paisley set the completed flower arrangement to the side. "Now, tell me what we'll need to order for the dance."

Laney filled Paisley in on the details and they brainstormed ideas about decorating for the backdrop. When Paisley left to make deliveries, Laney pulled her apron off the hook and tied it in place. The pink and purple flower print was stained in so many places that the pattern was unrecognizable. It was the only apron she had because she hadn't taken the time to find a new one. Straightening the pockets that were threadbare along the edges, Laney pulled off a loose thread and thought about how she felt like an old apron in a new place.

There was something bothering her that she hadn't realized before. She had left Echo Ridge, but so had Billy. He didn't come back right after college like he'd always planned. Did his plans change because of her, or would things have unfolded the same way? Strange how life twisted and turned into journeys she'd never anticipated. Laney blew out a breath and clipped the stems of the dark red roses that would go into the next arrangement. Paisley was right that Laney had a chance to clear the air with Billy by working with him on this project. But if she followed through with the plans for the homecoming dance, she might be walking right back into the trouble she'd stirred up with Billy in the first place.

It was a moment of weakness, Billy decided. He leaned forward and peered out the windshield of his truck, he was in trouble now. The sun rose high in the sky, nearing lunchtime and Billy was famished. He'd only had an apple for breakfast and that had probably contributed to the fuzzy images pounding his brain. Every image was Laney, bringing back another memory that they'd made together. He didn't like the way his heart winced with pain every time he thought of Laney. What was he thinking? Agreeing to work with Laney would be pure torture. He knew that, but when she'd bit her bottom lip and looked at him with those big brown eyes, he'd collapsed, just like the treehouse he'd tried to build Laney so long ago. Perhaps that was a metaphor for his life. It seemed the things that he spent the most time working on had collapsed into a jumbled mess when Laney left, but now that he was back in Echo Ridge things were going great. He was building a business and a life for himself that he could be proud of.

Billy pulled into Suzy Gibson's driveway. The three-story house was over a hundred years old and last spring he'd patched up the roof and one of the holes in his heart when he'd reconnected with Suzy's granddaughter, Elise Gibson. There had been a spark there, but ultimately prince charming had come and swept her off her feet. Literally. Taking Elise out on a date had been a great first step in realizing that Billy's heart could go on in the town of Echo Ridge without Laney Richins. He needed to remember that. He picked up his phone to call Kelli and tell her that he couldn't help out on the project after all when someone rapped on his window.

Billy jerked and dropped his phone. Suzy stood next to his pickup with her white hair curled close to her scalp and one of her trademark smiles. Billy opened the door. "You startled me."

Suzy chuckled, her blue eyes sparkling. "I can see that."

Billy hopped out of his truck and closed the door. "I came by to check on your roof. That last thunderstorm blew some shingles off my parents' house and I'm sure it didn't let you alone."

Suzy put a hand on her hip and turned toward the

house. "You're probably right, but I don't want you to feel like you have to look after this old house."

"Well, I want to," Billy replied. "And I like visiting with you." His stomach growled loudly and he flinched, hoping Suzy couldn't hear it.

"Hungry?" She took his arm. "You must have something awful powerful going on in that brain of yours if it can ignore a hunger tug like that. Why don't you come inside and have lunch with me?"

"Oh no, I don't want to impose."

"Nonsense. Besides we both know you can't turn down my famous chicken salad."

Billy held up his hands. "I surrender."

Suzy cackled and Billy found himself joining her laughter and feeling lighter as he climbed her porch steps. Suzy's kitchen felt like home and Billy found himself relaxing a bit as she bustled around, dishing up his lunch. The chicken salad was the perfect consistency and served over croissant rolls that were irresistibly flaky. Billy ate two and drank a glass of sweet tea with Suzy urging him to eat more.

"You're working too hard again," Suzy said. "You need to take time to enjoy life, settle down and raise a family."

"First you tell me I'm working too hard and then you tell me to go out and find more work. Which is it?"

"Both, and don't sass me." Suzy wagged her finger. "I

know you were sweet on Elise, but now that your heart's beating again, don't let it stop." She squeezed his arm. "And don't think that anyone believes for a minute that your soul mate hasn't come back to rescue you from your loneliness."

Billy snorted. She couldn't possibly be referring to Laney as his soulmate. "No offense, but last I checked soulmates aren't supposed to destroy someone's soul."

Now it was Suzy's time to snort. "As if a young pup like you even knows what he's talking about. You had a scrape. Clean it up, put on a bandage and don't let life pass you by because you're too busy worrying over a little scrape."

Billy put a hand over his heart. "Ow, I don't remember you being quite so blunt with me before."

Suzy winked. "Somebody needs to tell it like it is."

"Why is everyone trying so hard to interfere with my love life?" First Kelli and her homecoming dance schemes and now the seemingly harmless Suzy Gibson. Billy was half-scared of stopping by his parents' house.

"You speak as if you have a love life," Suzy retorted.

Billy laughed. "Now you're just being mean."

Suzy laughed with him. "Maybe, but at seventy-two I'm still sharp. Now quit moping and go get to work with Laney."

She was referring to Laney. How was it that the entire town of Echo Ridge was aware of her return and was now watching his every move? "I've already been forced to work with her, but I was just about to call Kelli and tell her I can't."

"Why would you do a fool thing like that?" Suzy rapped her knuckles on the table.

"Because Laney and I have too much history . . . and I don't know, she gets under my skin."

Suzy pursed her lips. "I've seen that look before, and if it means what I think it does then you should stop talking and listen to your heart. Not the wounded part that's trying to hold a pity party, either. Listen to the part pumping blood to your brain and figure out why she's getting under your skin."

Billy took his dishes to the sink. "Thanks again for lunch. I'll go check out your roof now."

"You're a good man. While you're busy running up the ladder away from this meddlesome woman, remember that second chances are God's way of helping us sort out this mess called life."

Billy nodded. "Isn't it time for your afternoon nap or something?"

Suzy tossed a napkin at him. "Oh, you. I have half a mind to call Laney up right now and invite her over for my famous chicken salad. She'd come, you know."

Billy laughed. "Remind me to come during your nap next time."

When he reached the top of Suzy's roof, he got to

work repairing a few missing and loose shingles. It took less than an hour but by the time he was finished, sweat was pouring off him. If he stayed busy enough, maybe he wouldn't have to think about Laney. After he showered off, he'd call Kelli and give her the bad news. No matter what Suzy said, Billy couldn't take a chance of getting tangled up with Laney again.

It was almost ten by the time Billy finally hit the shower that night. He was so tired that he decided he would put off calling Kelli until tomorrow. His muscles ached and the back of his neck was sunburned from working on Suzy's roof. He remembered what she'd said about second chances and wondered if he should at least try to work with Laney. Or maybe he could do most of the work and just give her a few assignments. They really wouldn't be working together if he could keep her out of his way. Billy smiled as he drifted out of consciousness. Yes, all he needed to do was keep Laney busy and everything would be fine.

CHAPTER 9

*L*aney wasn't sure who was more nervous on Oliver's first day of kindergarten, actually that wasn't true, she was definitely more nervous. Oliver was so excited to go to school that she'd barely had time to kiss him goodbye before he found his table and started chatting with another little boy.

She worried how he would do in all-day kindergarten, but when she picked him up just after three o'clock, Oliver had a grin that reached toward his ears.

"Mom, I love school! It's the best ever and Mrs. Jensen said we're going to read more stories on the rug tomorrow!" Oliver hugged Laney and kept talking as she helped him into the car.

Laney found herself grinning to match Oliver as he told her about recess, lunch, stories, and more recess.

"I'm so glad you had a good day. I think it's going to be a wonderful school year."

"Yep, and Adam is going to play on the slides with me."

"I used to love the slides too." Laney kept an eye on Oliver in her rearview mirror as she drove. He had a rooster tail that had popped back up during the day. His brown eyes danced with enthusiasm and Laney felt her heart warm to know that things were going to be okay in Echo Ridge for her little family.

"Hey, Mom, you missed our turn."

"We need to return our library books, so I'm heading to the library first."

"Okay, can we check if they have more Berenstain Bear books?"

"We sure can." Laney pulled into a space in front of the library.

She grabbed her stack of books and paused when she saw Britta walk out the front doors with Anika Rodriguez. The two women laughed and Anika placed a hand on her rounded stomach. Laney swallowed back the desire burning inside to give Oliver a brother or sister. She had loved growing up with her brothers and sister and had always planned to have three or four kids. That was back when she was writing out her life in her diary. Things didn't turn out as neatly off the page.

Laney got out of the car and unbuckled Oliver's seatbelt, shaking off haunting dreams of the past. Her phone rang and she hurried around to the front seat to answer it.

"Hi, Laney. This is Billy."

"Hey, how are you?" Laney tried to sound normal but her voice had a funny squeak at the end.

"I'm good. I'm calling because my sister suggested I change my attitude about working together, so I took her advice. I'm sorry if I was short with you the other day."

Laney put her hand on her throat, feeling the flush coming from her increasing heart rate. Billy was apologizing for not wanting to work with her? Did that mean he still had some feelings for her? "Oh, that's okay. I wasn't sure if it was the best idea either." Laney laughed to ease the tension around her heart.

"Well, if we're on the same team," Billy said, "I thought we should probably get together to figure out exactly what needs to happen to build this brig."

"Sure. I talked to Paisley and we've already placed orders for a few plants that will work nicely." She didn't mention that she'd been avoiding this phone call and had almost talked herself out of working with him. "What did you have in mind?"

"Well, I was going to try to set something up with you tomorrow, but maybe you ought to look behind you."

Laney froze and then turned around slowly. Billy was just getting out of his red truck. He held up two books and waved at her.

"Wait, I must be seeing things," Laney said. "For a second there, I thought I saw you, Billy Redford, holding *books* that I think might belong to the library."

Billy chuckled and his laugh sent familiar tingles down Laney's back. "It's me. I'm hanging up now, so come talk to me."

Laney gripped her phone and took a slow breath, before sliding it into her back pocket. She helped Oliver from the car and let him carry a few of the books. When she looked up, Billy smiled and her stomach did a double back flip. "Billy, you remember my son Oliver?"

Billy leaned over and held out his hand. "Of course. Hello, Oliver. How old are you?"

Oliver held up his hand with fingers outstretched and a big smile. "I'm five already!"

"Five? That's great. I bet your mom feels old having a five-year-old in the house."

Laney narrowed her eyes at Billy but Oliver spoke before she could reply.

"Yep. She's kind of old, but she's really pretty 'cause she's my mom."

"That's true on both counts." Billy's face flushed and Laney bit her lip to keep from laughing. He nodded toward the library. "Funny thing seeing you here."

They both knew he was teasing her. Laney had always loved to read and had coaxed Billy into reading several books that he would never admit to. The memory sparked something that gave her another idea. Maybe there was a way she could get through this assignment and come out on the other side with some semblance of a friendship with Billy. They walked toward the library and Oliver eagerly dropped his books into the return slot. Billy handed his over and Oliver dropped those in as well.

"I'm sorry I didn't call you before now," Billy said. "I've been working late every night."

"That's okay. We've had plenty to do to get ready for the first day of school. Oliver was so excited."

Billy grinned. "He does seem pretty happy. He's a cute kid."

"Thanks." Laney tucked a strand of hair behind her ear, trying to collect her thoughts. Billy had sounded sincere just now when he referred to Oliver. It wasn't surprising because she knew Billy was a good guy, it only caught her attention because of the stark contrast between him and her ex-husband Dane. He'd pretended he wanted kids until Laney discovered she was pregnant. It was only then that she began to see how selfish he was, and then it was too late.

"Mom, can we find my books now?" Oliver tugged

on her hand, pointing toward the stairs that led to the children's section.

"Yes, let's go check them out." Laney turned to Billy. "Would you like to help us find a Berenstain Bear's book Oliver hasn't checked out already?"

"I'd love to," Billy replied. "Hey, Oliver, my favorite is *The Messy Room*. How about you?"

"*The Gimmies!*" Oliver hurried down the stairs, not waiting for a response.

Laney and Billy chuckled, and then Laney tripped over her own feet. She grabbed onto the railing at the same time Billy pulled her upright. "Oops! My feet got ahead of themselves."

He put a hand on the small of her back. "Be careful, Laney. The books will still be there when we catch up to Oliver."

Laney shook her head. "*The Messy Room* might be gone though."

Billy laughed and for a second she saw the boy she used to know. The mischievous gleam in his crystal blue eyes begged to be let free. She was ultra-aware of his hand near her waist and the warmth of his fingertips through her cotton blouse. She cleared her throat. "On the brig. I think if we keep things simple and use lots of greenery, you'll only have to build the platform. Maybe that will keep the costs down?"

To his credit, Billy took the change in subject in stride. They stood near a stack of books while Oliver hunted for his favorites. "I was thinking the same thing. Maybe a three-sided box with an opening for the bars. Not sure the best way to build the bars."

"What about PVC pipe spray-painted black?" Laney suggested.

Billy snapped his fingers. "That's an excellent idea. Can you handle that part and I'll work on building the box?"

"I guess so."

"Good." Billy nodded. "Maybe you could drop the pipe by once it's dry and I'll attach it."

"It would probably be easier to build it at your shop. I don't really have the tools for this sort of project."

Billy hesitated. "I don't know. My schedule has been so crazy."

"Why don't you give me a call when you have a few minutes on Thursday night? And we'll want to measure and cut the pipe before I paint it, otherwise it will chip the paint."

"But what about Oliver? Doesn't he have an early bedtime?"

"Yes, but I can always have my mom or dad run over for a few minutes if it's past that.

"Billy, you do realize that the Homecoming dance is next Saturday. As in just over a week from now?"

"Well, yeah, but—"

"Save your buts for Kelli. I promised Alex I'd help. Paisley is willing to do extra. I'm not letting them down. We can do this." She tilted her head, studying Billy. "Right?"

Billy sighed. "Right. I'll call you Thursday or Friday when I'm ready for the bars to be installed on our brig."

The way he said it made it sound like he was the one who would be imprisoned. Laney shrugged, it made her head hurt trying to figure out what was going on inside Billy's. She crouched next to Oliver and began thumbing through the books. "Okay, I'll talk to you then."

To her surprise, Billy walked to the other side of Oliver, bent down and pulled out a book that was turned the wrong way on the shelf. He handed it to Laney. "Have fun reading, Oliver." Billy patted him on the back as he walked past.

Laney flipped the picture book over and laughed when she recognized the cover of The Berenstain Bears and *The Messy Room.* "How did he do that?" she asked Oliver. She turned toward the stairs but Billy was gone, leaving her amidst books which usually brought her comfort. Right then, all the words in the world couldn't help her understand Billy. He had smiled, chatted, and acted friendly until Laney brought up working together on the Homecoming project. His mood had changed and he'd acted like he didn't want to work with her. Was he really that uncomfortable being around her? Laney pressed her lips together as she flipped through the pages of her favorite childhood book. Memories of happy times with Billy swirled around the edges of her consciousness.

illy's plan to avoid Laney had failed miserably. She'd overcome every objection he'd brought up and she was insistent that they couldn't let down the Homecoming committee. In the end, he'd agreed to work with her at his shop. The worst part was that he was looking forward to working with her. She was vivacious as always, with fun ideas that popped into her brain and out her mouth before she had a chance to filter them. Laney carried an energy with her everywhere she went that spilled onto those around her. Billy had always loved spending time with her, which was exactly the reason he shouldn't have agreed to work with her. He was opening the door to more hurt and pain.

He wondered if Laney could have changed. Maybe

he wouldn't get hurt by mending the friendship they'd once shared. He'd noticed how sweet she was with her little boy. She was patient with him and constantly smiled in his direction. Oliver looked a lot like Laney, with a light smattering of freckles over his nose and chocolate brown eyes. Billy wondered what the story was behind Laney's ex-husband. It was strange that everyone seemed to be pushing him toward Laney, but no one had mentioned the man from her past. Billy made a note to check into her history. He couldn't think of any reason that someone would be dumb enough to give up on Laney and Oliver, so the guy must be a real loser.

Billy groaned. He needed something to get his mind off Laney and her son. As if hearing his thoughts, his phone rang. Billy grinned and answered the welcome distraction.

"Hello, Billy," Evangeline Hyatt said. Her rich voice reminded him of the many times he'd visited Winston and her on their farm.

"How are you doing?" Billy asked.

"Well if you must know I just can't get this thought out of my head," Evangeline grumbled.

"What is it?"

"I think you need to live here. The barn, the corrals, the greenhouse—all of it needs so much work and it needs to be from someone who loves it and loves the work. That's you, isn't it?"

Billy opened his mouth, closed it, and pulled to the side of the road.

"Billy? This darn phone."

"No, I'm still here. I just, uh, what did you say?"

"My place is for sale and you need to buy it," Evangeline said.

Billy chuckled. "I would love to buy your place, but my business is still in its infancy and I don't think the bank would loan me that kind of money."

"You're right, they probably wouldn't, but I would," Evangeline replied.

Billy's hands shook and he pushed the phone closer to his ear. "I'm headed your way, Evangeline. Can we talk about this in person?"

Evangeline chuckled. "Got your attention then? Sure, come on over. I'll get the sodas ready."

Billy sped on his way out of town, his mind bursting with the possibilities that Evangeline had just opened up. He didn't want to get his hopes up, but they had already soared up to the puffy clouds in the clear blue sky. He'd dreamed of living in a place like the Hyatt's' farm for most of his life. He grinned and whispered a prayer, "Lord, if there's any way I can make this work, please show me how."

As he approached the Hyatts' house, he saw in it the

immense possibilities and the incredible amount of work it would require. He understood why Evangeline wanted to sell it, but he hadn't even called the realtor to find out the asking price. Billy hopped out of his truck and hurried to the front door. He knocked twice and Evangeline opened the door with a smile.

"Well, that was quick."

"I was close by," Billy replied.

"Come on in." Evangeline motioned for him to follow.

Billy followed her into the sunlit kitchen and sat down at the round dining table. The kitchen cabinets were oak, and everything about the house looked outdated. With a few cans of paint and repairs, he could give the house a facelift.

"Already fixing things in that brain of yours?" Evangeline handed Billy an old-fashioned root beer in a glass bottle.

"There is a lot of potential here. A lot of work." He popped the top and sipped the cool liquid.

"I had a dream a couple days ago and it wouldn't let me go." Evangeline sat next to him. "Yesterday I met with my realtor and drew up some papers for a rent-to-own opportunity. I know you've loved this place since you and Laney were little tykes and I'd like to help you."

Billy noticed the pile of papers on the kitchen table. "I can't lie. This makes my heart about beat right out of my chest. I do love this place, but you need to take care of yourself first."

"Oh pooh. I'm an old lady and we both know I can't hold a shovel like I used to." Evangeline leaned forward. "I'm well taken care of because I married a good man. Winston planned ahead. We talked about this a few years ago and decided that we would retire to a smaller place." Evangeline paused and tapped the tabletop. "The only part we didn't plan on was him leaving here first."

"I'm sorry," Billy said. "He was a great man. We all miss him."

Evangeline patted his hand. "You're a good boy, Billy Redford. I want you to take these papers with you and look through them. Take the time you need to think about it. I'm not giving anything away here. I'm just trying to do what's right by this place because it needs a certain kind of person to be a steward over it."

Billy liked the way Evangeline spoke as if her farm were a living and breathing thing because in his mind it had always been more than just a house and buildings. "Thank you. I'd love to take a look and see if I can make this happen. I love this place."

"I know." Evangeline pushed the packet of papers closer to him. "Now before you go, tell me about your business. What's been keeping you so busy lately?"

They ended up chatting for another thirty minutes before Billy had to head out to his next appointment.

The packet of papers on his seat seemed to have a heart-beat of its own as Billy drove through Echo Ridge, waiting until he parked to look at them. When he opened up the sheaf of papers, he saw the original asking price followed by the new purchase plan. It was more than generous. He would rent-to-own the property for three years and then he would take out a loan for the rest of the mortgage. During that time he would make repairs and improve the property and because of that work, his monthly rent was half what it should have been. All he needed right now was ten-thousand dollars cash to put toward the lease agreement.

Billy stacked the papers on his seat, leaning forward against the steering wheel. For some reason, God was smiling on him, giving him a chance to live out his dreams on the Hyatts' farm. There wouldn't be a second chance for something like this. Billy knew that he had to find a way to get the down payment and make Evangeline's dream for him come true. When he raised his head, his eyes widened, but then he shook his head. For a moment he'd seen himself on the Hyatt's farm working alongside Laney and Oliver. The sun had been streaming down, casting its light on Laney's creamy skin and dotting Oliver's face with more freckles and they were smiling at him. Billy rubbed his hand over his forehead. Too much excitement for one day and the late August heat was playing tricks on his mind.

He got out of the truck and buckled his tool belt. The vision rippled along the edges of his consciousness like a heat wave and Billy didn't push it aside. He held onto it as he worked through the day, trying to figure out what God wanted him to know.

CHAPTER 11

Thursday morning Laney got a text from Billy.

Can you meet me at the shop at 7? You can bring Oliver if it's not too late.

Laney smiled and reread the text three times before she replied: *Yes!*

That simple text changed the rest of the day for Laney because Billy had invited Oliver. He couldn't understand what that meant to her, because he didn't know her ex-husband Dane Peterson. The man who had lied to her, cheated, broken her heart, and signed papers to prove that he didn't care if he ever saw Oliver again. Laney snipped the stem of a Gerber daisy and reminded herself not to think about Dane. His utter contempt for fatherhood was a blessing in disguise. As long as she had Oliver, Dane wasn't interested in interfering in her life because he was too worried that he might have to actually act like a father.

Laney tied a ribbon around the glass vase holding three pink Gerbera daisies. It was a simple arrangement, but so beautiful in its simplicity. It reminded her of Echo Ridge because Laney had begun to notice the beauty of her small town and the people in it. She still had doubts at times about whether it was the best place for Oliver's future, but she chose to focus on reality instead of doubts. The reality of her hometown was that it was the perfect place for her and Oliver to be right now.

After work, Laney and Oliver cooked up salmon and broccoli with jasmine rice and Oliver cleared his plate before Laney had even finished asking him about school. Then her mom called and invited them over for homemade ice cream.

"Mom, I'd love to but I'm supposed to be working on building this backdrop for the homecoming dance tonight."

"Oh? Is that with Billy Redford?"

"Yes, but it's just wood and nails, nothing else." Laney tried to keep her voice even because she'd been thinking about working with Billy all day and she hadn't thought about wood or nails once.

"Okay, if it's just work that doesn't sound like much fun for Oliver. Why don't you drop him off on your way over?" Josi asked. "He can play here and I'll take him back to your house and get him to bed on time."

Laney considered her mother's offer. What she said was true, it would be easier to get stuff done without him running underfoot. But what about Billy? He'd invited Oliver, so what would he think when Laney showed up by herself?

"Don't overthink this. Just bring Oliver over," Josi interrupted her thoughts.

"You're right, Mom. We'll be over in just a few." Laney ended the call and hurried to get ready. She pulled her hair back into a ponytail and touched up her makeup. After a full day of work she didn't want to look like death warmed over, so she put on a pair of gold hoop earrings. She told herself she just wanted to look presentable, she wasn't trying to look nice for Billy.

Thankfully, Josi didn't say anything about Laney's appearance or her hurry to get over to Billy's. She did share a knowing mother look that Laney chose to ignore as she drove toward Billy's shop. Laney arrived just before seven and took in two deep breaths of air-conditioned coolness before stepping into the late evening heat. As she approached the shop she heard the whine of a buzz saw so she decided to let herself in.

Sawdust danced through the air pushed by a high-powered fan in the corner. Billy bent over the saw cutting wood planks. His dark green t-shirt pulled taut against his broad shoulders and Laney smiled at the light coating of sawdust on the back of his head. It almost blended in with his dark blond hair, which was trimmed short. When they were in high school he'd often let his hair grow out until it was a mass of curls and waves. Laney had often threatened him with a pair of scissors if he didn't get a proper haircut. She smiled at the memory and Billy turned around at the same moment.

"Oh, I didn't hear you come in."

Laney straightened and licked her lips. "I heard the saw, so I let myself in."

"That's okay. I'm glad you could make it." Billy looked behind her. "Where's Oliver?"

"Oh, my mom called and invited him for homemade ice cream just before I left. I have to admit I was tempted to stay." Laney patted her stomach.

Billy gave her an easy smile. "You should've and you should've nabbed a dish for me. Oliver's lucky."

"Now that would've been a good idea."

"Well, tell Oliver hello for me. In fact, I'd better give you this now before I forget." Billy walked over to a table scattered with papers and tools. He moved aside a couple papers and picked up a green hardback book. He walked toward Laney, holding it out. "I was going through a box of old books and found this. I wanted to give it to him."

Laney took the book and gasped. "It's the Honey Hunt!"

Billy grinned. "Yep. Thought you might remember that one."

Laney examined one of the first Berenstain Bear books written. It was a hardcover picture book and it looked to be a first edition. Laney had looked for it in the library when Oliver had begun to get interested in the famous bear family, but they didn't have it. She hugged the book and felt warmth rise up her throat with emotion that threatened to spill over. What was wrong with her? She swallowed. "This is so sweet of you, Billy. Thank you." She reached out and squeezed his hand.

Billy nodded. "I'm glad you like it." He stepped away from her, letting her hand fall. "Let me show you what I'm thinking for our brig."

Laney put the book in her purse and set it on a chair by the door. She shouldn't be surprised by Billy's actions because he was just being himself, but it had been too long since she'd been around a man who genuinely cared about her *and* her son. She walked over to where Billy stood in front of a piece of plywood.

"This is the base." He stepped onto the plywood and held up his hands. "We'll put three sides on and the couple can walk in from the back."

"Isn't that kind of small?" Laney pointed to where he stood.

"Well, that's the point. It's a brig, not a sitting room."

Laney rolled her eyes. She stepped onto the plywood next to Billy. "Yes, but what about group pictures? We want to make sure that a group of ten or twelve can be in the picture."

Billy shook his head. "That would take too much material. One, maybe two couples can be in the brig at a time. The rest will have to stand around the sides."

"I guess that'll work, but you know we'll have to be there to make sure they don't climb on top and break it."

"Kelli already asked me if we'd be willing to take a shift since we'll have to be there to set it up anyway." Billy looked at the ground. "I kind of forgot to tell you about it."

Laney nudged him with her shoulder, pushing him off balance. "You kind of forgot?"

Billy stepped off the plywood. "I remembered now, didn't I?"

Laney rolled her eyes. "Okay, what else do we need to do to get this thing built?"

"Do you like power tools?" Billy waggled his eyebrows as he picked up a nail gun.

Laney laughed. "Quit showing off and let's get to work."

They continued to banter as they worked together and Laney found herself wondering what had happened to the grumpy and hesitant Billy she thought she was going to find. Maybe all the history they'd shared had made him uncomfortable until he realized that she was still Laney even if they had both changed.

Laney helped measure and mark another sheet of plywood and then held it steady while Billy cut it with his electric saw. He stopped and mopped at his forehead with a handkerchief. "You're actually pretty handy. Thanks for the help tonight."

Laney put a hand on her hip. "What's that supposed to mean?"

"Just what it sounds like." Billy didn't hesitate. "I sort of thought you might just break out the pom poms and cheer me on while I worked."

Laney shook her head. "You always were a tease."

"And you always were a cheerleader."

"You liked me just fine back then."

Billy's face flushed and he frowned. "Help me hold this side up and I'll see if this is going to work."

Laney let him change the subject because the tension in the room was making the back of her neck itch. Billy was quiet as he attached pieces of wood to the plywood. He stood and dusted off his pants. "There. Those 2 x 2s will make it so we can snap this thing together pretty quick. It's heavy, so we'll get some help to bring it in but I think it'll work."

"I guess I can take the measurements for the PVC pipe now."

"Yep. I'll get some plumber's tape to fasten the pipes to the plywood here." He pointed to the opening they'd made for the prison."

"Plumber's tape?"

"It's thin metal strips that you can use to fasten all kinds of things in place. You'll see."

"Will I?"

"Yeah, do you think you can get the stuff and come back tomorrow?"

"Sure." Laney nodded and stuck her hands into her pockets. For a minute there when Billy was teasing her about being a cheerleader it had felt like old times, but then he'd turned cold again. "Billy? Is everything okay?"

"Yeah, why?" He didn't look at her as he cleaned up his workspace.

Even though eight years had passed, Laney could still read him like a book. There was something bothering him because he hadn't looked her in the eye. Billy didn't make eye contact when he wasn't sure how to answer a question that might have an uncomfortable answer.

"Billy. Look at me."

He clipped his measuring tape into his tool belt and turned toward Laney. The moment his blue eyes connected with hers, Laney's heart jolted into motion. Billy took a step toward her, his eyes never leaving hers. Laney swallowed, feeling a rush of heat bloom across her skin. He took another step forward, close enough that Laney smelled his cologne—sweet and spice, earthy yet fresh. It was different than she remembered, but somehow the same.

"I'm looking at you, Laney," Billy whispered. "I don't know how to do this. When I'm around you, I remember things that we used to do. I remember *everything* and I'm not sure if I ever knew you."

All she could do was blink and try to breathe. "You knew me better than I knew myself."

He shook his head. "That's not true. We both had a lot of growing up to do, but now you're back here and I'm not sure how to treat you. I don't know if you're going to stay or leave. I didn't want to work on this project with you, but I couldn't get out of it."

Laney took a step back, surprised at his confession. "I'm sorry. I should've realized how uncomfortable this would make you."

"It's okay. Let's get this finished." He broke eye contact and turned toward the door. "I should probably let you get back. Be sure Oliver knows that book is from me."

Laney smiled. "I will." She wanted to say something more, but Billy had already walked across the shop, closing the discussion. She picked up her purse and headed out to her car.

Turning the air conditioner on full blast, Laney drove home slowly, replaying the night with Billy. They had been having so much fun, teasing, laughing and working together until Billy turned into an ice block with closed off feelings. Laney leaned her head back against the seat as she turned the corner to her house. They couldn't skirt around the issue anymore. She needed to make things right, to let Billy know that she was sorry for hurting him. But how could she do that without opening up the door to the possibility of more hurt?

CHAPTER 12

Billy headed to work Friday at five in the morning to beat the heat that wouldn't let up. By ten o'clock he was ravenous and his eggs and bacon had burned off long ago. He headed to Fay's Café for an early lunch. Lucky for him, it was early enough that no one else in Echo Ridge was thinking of lunch so he was in and out of Fay's in twenty minutes. He carried a twisted soda out to his truck and set it next to his tool-box. He was about to pull out his phone to check his messages when a man stepped out from the side of a silver SUV.

"So, you're Billy Redford?" The man's hair was almost black and he looked Mediterranean, but Billy hadn't detected an accent.

Billy glanced at the vinyl logo on his truck and then back at the man. He nodded and held out his hand.

"Yes, I own Redbuilt Construction. What can I do for you?"

The man didn't shake his hand. His eyes narrowed and his upper lip curled. "You can stay away from my wife."

Billy pulled his hand back. "Your wife?"

"Laney Peterson."

"I don't know anyone by that name." Billy wrinkled his nose, quickly assessing the bulldog in front of him. The guy had to be Dane Peterson, Laney's ex-husband. "I know a Laney Richins though."

The man frowned. "You know who I'm talking about. Just because you and Laney ran around in high school doesn't mean you can pick up where you left off."

"Oh, is that what you think is happening?" Billy raised an eyebrow. "I thought I was helping my sister with the homecoming committee and Laney happened to be on that same committee."

"Laney told me all about you." Dane pointed at him, jabbing his finger with every other word. "Small town boy. Small town dreams. She never wanted any part of that. If she's back here, it's to lick her wounds and gather some pity before she runs off again."

Billy's nerves were like live wires under his skin—a bomb about to explode. He breathed in slowly through his nose. "Like I said, I don't know any Laney Peterson. The Laney I know is a good person, a good mother, and a good friend. I guess if leaving is what Laney decides is right for her, she'll do it. What I find interesting is the fact that you're here in Echo Ridge, claiming you have a wife named Laney Peterson. Have you checked with missing persons?"

Dane clenched his jaw and the muscle in his cheek twitched. "Don't toy with me. When Laney gets tired of you, she'll come back to the real man." He pointed at his chest.

Billy nodded. "Good to know. Guess I could save her some time and let her know you're in town, you know, in case she's looking for the real man."

Dane narrowed his eyes. "You think she sees anything in you—a blue collar worker?"

Billy raised his chin. He'd had more than enough. He popped the lid of his toolbox and picked up his sledgehammer, turning slowly to face Dane. "What was that? I thought you said you were just leaving. Would you like me to help you out?" He took a step forward and Dane jumped back.

"Are you threatening me?"

Billy gripped the hammer and raised it two inches. Then he lifted a finger and tugged at the collar of his t-shirt. "I'm just trying to get a little work done, but if you need help finding the interstate, let me know."

Dane opened his mouth and then clamped it shut. Billy leaned forward slightly and was rewarded when

Dane spun on his heel and left. Billy thought about smiling, but the words that Dane had spat cut like barbs on a wire. Where did the bluster and lies end and the truth begin in Dane's words?

Billy climbed into his truck and fired it up, cranking the air conditioner to full blast. All day long, Billy had dodged thoughts of Laney and how things had ended last night. He felt bad about putting her on the spot and he was already practicing what he might say when he saw her tonight to work on the backdrop. His phone beeped and Billy saw a text come through from Laney.

Hey, I won't be able to make it tonight. I'm working late with Paisley for a wedding tomorrow.

Should he tell her about her ex-husband? Billy wasn't sure what her relationship was like with Dane. Maybe he was there to visit Oliver. Billy decided to wait until he saw Laney in person, which needed to be sooner than later.

Can we work on it Saturday?

Yes, I get off at 2. I have an idea. Can you meet me at Second Chances at 2:30?

Billy pulled his bottom lip through his teeth, wondering what Laney had planned. *The thrift store? Why there?*

Trust me.

Billy bit the inside of his cheek. Trusting Laney was a

big step, but he was willing to keep walking forward. He typed in a reply: *K, see you then.*

He scanned the parking lot. There was no sign of Dane Peterson. He still wasn't sure how to handle the situation. Billy drained his soda and pulled out onto the street. He drove slowly through town, accelerating as he hit the main highway outside of Echo Ridge. He'd taken a few days to study out Evangeline Hyatt's offer and it felt like the right thing to do. The down payment would take some time to raise but he wanted to give Evangeline his answer in person.

Every time Billy entered the boundary of the Hyatts' property, he felt peaceful, like he'd stepped back in time. It felt like home, and for that reason alone he wanted to make this work. Billy knocked on the front door and waited for Evangeline to answer. The door squeaked as she pulled it open.

"Well, hello, Billy. I'm glad to see you." She stepped aside. "Come on in out of that sticky heat."

"Gladly." Billy clutched the folder of paperwork Evangeline had given him and stepped inside. "I won't stay long. I just wanted to come by and tell you that I've made a decision."

"I sure am glad to hear that," Evangeline replied. "It's the right thing for you and your family."

Billy opened his mouth, but she'd snatched the words before he could speak.

Evangeline laughed. "Don't look so surprised. You don't think God would tease an old woman like me, do you? He told me what to do and here you are."

Billy grinned. "It does make things rest easier on my mind."

"Have a seat." Evangeline motioned to the front sitting room. "I was about to have some fresh-squeezed lemonade, so maybe you'll join me?"

"I wouldn't miss it." Billy sat facing the picture window that overlooked the pasture where he counted six cows grazing. When Evangeline brought him the lemonade, they both sipped quietly for a moment, enjoying the view.

"It's beautiful, isn't it?" she whispered.

"It is." Billy put his glass down. "I mean to make this happen. The down payment is giving me somewhat of a headache right now because I've tried to be careful with my business finances, but there have been a lot of expenses I couldn't foresee as a new owner."

"Trust God. Believe past the fear and doubt and know that He will help you get to the place you're supposed to be." Evangeline gazed out the window as she spoke, her white hair shining under the overhead light.

"That's good advice," Billy said. "I'll take it. Things are going great in my business so I'm sure the bank will loan me the ten grand if needed, but I'd like to take a couple weeks to see what I can come up with in the meantime." Billy slid a paper out of the folder. "I've signed this and attached a check for the earnest money."

"Thank you. This means a lot to me to know that Winston's heart can still beat in this land he worked so hard to cultivate."

Billy savored those words and his own heart beat steadily in rhythm to all the possibilities that could be in his life, in this place that he was meant to be.

CHAPTER 13

The Friday before homecoming week was notoriously busy, but even Paisley hadn't been able to anticipate the onslaught of orders on top of a weekend wedding. Laney's feet felt like cinderblocks by the time she cleaned up the shop. At seven o'clock Paisley called her husband and sister to finish up a few things and shooed Laney out the door. Laney stepped outside and took a deep breath. The air hung heavy with humidity and a bead of sweat trickled down her back. A cold shower and iced tea would be a welcome treat after the long day she'd put in. At least Oliver had called with the help of his grandma and reported another successful day of kindergarten. Laney smiled when she thought of his little voice pitching high with excitement as he told her about the assembly they'd had with snakes and monkeys. Echo Ridge Elementary was an excellent school. One more reason Laney was happy with her choice to return home. She stepped from the shadow of the building toward her car in the parking lot and froze.

A man leaned against her car, dark sunglasses, darker hair, and dressed in trendy golf shorts and a polo shirt. He straightened when he saw her approaching—the last person she thought she'd see in Echo Ridge. Dane Peterson.

"I should've known you'd come running back to podunkville," Dane said.

Laney stopped ten feet from him. "What are you doing here?"

"No, hello? No, how are you doing?" Dane took two steps forward.

"Stop!" Laney held out her hand. "I asked you a question and I expect an answer."

Dane held up his hands and took a step back. "I thought it was obvious. I'm here to see you."

"Why?"

Dane laughed and the sound was like chalkboard scratching to Laney's nerves. That condescending laugh had won more battles for Dane than he'd ever know, but no more. She knew every one of his manipulative tricks.

"Honey, it's been long enough. Why don't you let me take you home?"

"I am home." Laney pulled her keys from her purse.

"Please move away from my car. I've had a long day and I don't want to talk to you."

"You can't be happy here," Dane replied as if she hadn't spoken. "I remember everything you told me about this stifling little town. Don't delude yourself by coming back here and hooking up with your high school sweetheart."

Laney flinched. "Are you spying on me?"

"I looked up Redbuilt Construction." Dane arched an eyebrow. "I knew Billy wasn't telling the truth. He told me that you two weren't carrying on—something about the Homecoming committee. But you," he pointed a finger at her, "I can see that you think something is there." He clicked his tongue. "Poor little Laney, falling into the same sad story."

"Shut up, Dane!" Laney tried to push past him, but he grabbed onto her arm.

"Will you just give me ten minutes? I really need to talk to you."

"Let go of me." Laney wrenched her arm free and unlocked her car. "Do you honestly think I would ever be stupid enough to spend one more minute with you?"

"Now, honey, you don't mean that." Dane put his hand on her door frame, leaning toward her.

Laney glared at Dane. "You haven't even mentioned our son. It's like he doesn't even exist. Well, guess what? You and me," she motioned between them, "that's what doesn't exist. The only real thing in my life is Oliver and just like you agreed before a judge, you won't ever see him again." Laney shoved Dane back and scrambled toward her car. Thankfully he didn't follow her. She jumped inside the car that emanated heat waves and locked her door. Gunning the engine, she peeled out of the parking lot, sweat pouring off her until her legs stuck to the seats.

Dane was telling the truth. He had come to Echo Ridge to see her, not their son. Laney's chin trembled and angry tears fell onto her cheeks. She was over him, but she hated that he could still get to her. The things he'd said about her and Echo Ridge seared her consciousness. Words from her past were weapons in Dane's mouth—that's how it always was with him. He took her words and twisted them to use however he wanted to get his way. Laney swiped the tears away. There might be some truth to Dane's words but she couldn't let him get to her.

Laney looked for any sign of Dane in her neighborhood, but he wasn't there. She took extra time to cuddle with Oliver and allow his sweet smiles to erase the ugliness of Dane's words.

"Mommy, will you read me Billy's book again tonight?" Oliver asked. He had the green hardback book tucked under his arm.

"I'd love to." Laney took Oliver's hand and they sat

on his bed to read. They read *The Honey Hunt* twice before Laney insisted it was past Oliver's bedtime. He wanted to sleep with the book next to him on his pillow. Laney waited ten minutes and then snuck back in his room and snapped a picture with her phone. Her angelic son had one arm around the book as he slept. Laney's heart warmed with the meaning behind the book that Billy had given to her son. It meant that Billy had thought about her and Oliver after they were gone. He'd thought about Oliver enough to go through a box of books and pick one out that a kindergartner would love. It meant that Billy cared and that was something Laney couldn't ignore. Tomorrow she would clear the air between them and apologize for past hurts. Hopefully Billy would see that she was still someone worth knowing.

CHAPTER 14

When Laney pulled into the parking lot of the Second Chances thrift store, she immediately noticed Billy's red pickup. She was five minutes late, but Billy didn't look perturbed as he exited his truck. Maybe he'd also just arrived.

"Hi, Billy. How's your day going?"

Billy rubbed the back of his sunburned neck. "Started before five." He yawned and stretched his arms over his head. "I keep trying to beat the heat, but it's beating me."

"I hear ya, but I didn't start before five. The shop has been so busy today. With the wedding tonight and homecoming next week, Paisley is out of her mind trying to keep up with all the orders."

"So I'm still trying to figure out why you wanted to come to the thrift shop," Billy said.

"I was trying to think of ways to cut costs." Laney opened the front door. "Like I said, you have to trust me. I wanted to look around and see if there was anything that we could use for the pirate décor.

"I trust you. I'm here aren't I?"

Laney smiled and then she wrinkled her nose. For as long as she'd been coming to Second Chances, the thrift store had an unmistakable smell of mothballs, dust, and geriatric relics mixed together. They walked past rows of clothing ranging from baby to adult. Laney picked up a few faded bouquets of fake flowers.

"Something like this might work to fill in around the plants that Paisley is bringing in."

Billy shrugged. "Whatever you say, Boss."

"These look like they belong in a museum," Billy said. He held up an old radio and Laney laughed. Then she turned around and saw something that gave her a wonderful idea.

"That's it." Laney pointed at the rickety old crib.

"What?" Billy turned to see where Laney was pointing.

"It's perfect! We'll be able to use it for the brig. It's going to save us so much time."

"A crib? Laney, I understand that babies think it's a jail cell, but we're going for a pirate theme."

Laney swatted him with the fake flower bouquet. "It's perfect for the front of our brig. We can just put the two panels together and spray paint the whole thing."

Billy cocked his head to one side. "Hmm, you just might be right."

"Of course I'm right!" She grabbed hold of the crib railing. "Can you believe how much time I just saved us?"

Billy lifted the price tag and examined the handwritten amount of fifteen dollars. "Money too."

"Oh, I love finding great deals." Laney hugged Billy. He stiffened, and then hugged her back. "Sorry about that." She stepped out of his embrace, feeling her face flush.

Billy chuckled. "No need to apologize. It's been a long time. I almost forgot how excited you get about little things."

Laney wagged her finger at him. "It's the little things that make life great."

"I know. So should we buy this crib and load it into my truck?"

"Yep." She pulled the tag off the crib and headed for the register, leaving Billy to roll the crib forward.

The cashier glanced at Laney's stomach and then grinned at Billy. "Must be exciting times at your house."

"Oh no—" Billy started, but Laney interrupted him.

"It is. So much work to do before next weekend, but I'm sure we'll make it." Laney handed him the money, turned and winked at Billy and then shouldered her purse.

The cashier glanced at her stomach again and furrowed his brow. "Good luck with that."

The doors hadn't closed completely before Laney busted out laughing. "You should've seen your face."

Billy shook his head but he was laughing right along with her. "You should've seen his face. Next weekend." Billy rolled the crib alongside his pickup.

Laney laughed so hard that tears leaked from the corners of her eyes. She leaned against the truck and sighed. "Oh, that makes me feel younger than I am."

"He asked for it, I guess." Billy opened his tailgate and they hoisted the crib inside. "Want to come and help me get started on this?"

"Don't you have more work to do?" Laney tried to keep her voice normal. She wanted to go with Billy. Oliver was playing with his cousins today so it would be the perfect opportunity to finish up most of the building project.

"I'm on my lunch break until four. Remember, I've already put in a full day."

"I don't want to take up your lunch break, but I did already buy the black spray paint." Laney glanced at her car and back at Billy.

"Well, come on then. Follow me over."

"See you in a few." Laney hurried to her car and

smiled as she drove behind Billy and the wobbly crib in the back of his truck. When they got to his shop, she helped him unload the crib and grabbed two cans of black spray paint.

Billy handed her an Allen wrench with about ten different sizes. "See if you can find which one fits and we'll take this thing apart."

"Okay, thanks again for doing this, Billy. I know you're swamped with work," Laney said. "It means a lot to the kids. My nephew Alex thinks you're pretty cool."

"They're good kids," Billy replied. "And I'd say you're just as busy as me. Are you feeling like you're all settled in?"

"Just about." Laney tried another size on the Allen wrench set. "Oliver loves kindergarten and talks nonstop about his friends and his teacher. That is such a relief."

"I can imagine."

"Got it!" Laney held up the correct size Allen wrench and Billy moved to help her loosen the screws holding the crib frame in place.

Every time Billy came near her, Laney could smell his scent—clean with a spicy undertone. It was familiar. That scent reminded her of all the good times that they had working together on projects as kids and even during high school. She also noticed the way his cargo shorts fit just right hanging low with the tool belt strapped around his waist. Billy's skin was dark from working outside in the sun and the top of his head looked blonder than usual. For all the memories and good feelings there was still a strain between them and Laney really wanted to clear the air but she didn't know how to do it.

"Laney?"

"Huh?"

Billy chuckled. "I lost you there for a minute." Billy waved a hand near her face. "I asked what else you had planned for today, but you must have a lot on your mind."

Laney snapped back into focus. "I'm sorry. My mind keeps wandering." She took a breath. Now was as good a time as any to have a heart-to-heart with Billy. She bit her lip and forced herself to continue. "Billy, could I talk to you for a minute?"

"Sure." He set down the wrench and looked her in the eye. That should have made it easier, but it made it more difficult. When they were dating, Laney often got after him for not listening, or worse, talking too much about football. She remembered taking his face in her hands and telling him to look her in the eye and really listen to what she was saying. He had usually blown her off or kissed her, but that was a long time ago. Evidently, Billy had learned to be a good listener and that meant that he would hear everything she was about to say. "I've really enjoyed working with you on this project."

Billy nodded, but didn't say anything.

"But I've noticed that you've seemed sort of uncomfortable around me—even angry when you first showed up to the meeting. I wanted to say that I don't blame you." She gripped the edge of the crib railing and continued looking at Billy who was still listening intently. "So much has changed since we were kids and I —well, I wanted to apologize for how things ended that summer after high school. I was wrong."

"Laney, you don't have to apologize." Billy put his hand over hers. "We were kids. What did we know?"

"But I did know." Laney licked her lips. "I knew I was hurting you but I couldn't stop myself from running. I was selfish."

"You were eighteen," Billy replied. "Find me an eighteen year old who isn't selfish. I was selfish too. I wanted things to work out between us because I had big plans, but you know what? Those plans weren't right. We both had to make our own way and learn our own lessons."

"But I could've handled things better." Laney turned her hand over and clasped his. "I was wrong about leaving Echo Ridge behind, about you—about everything. I'm here to stay."

Billy glanced at their hands and then back at her. "Thank you for telling me this. I'm sorry that I haven't been acting normal. It really took me off guard when you moved back to Echo Ridge. I don't think I realized how much of the past I was still carrying with me."

"Me, too."

"Crazy that you can still read me. We haven't been around each other for almost a decade," Billy said. "How did you know I was upset?"

Laney laughed. "How could I not know when you were shooting darts with your eyes?"

Billy grinned and his cheeks reddened.

"I hope you can forgive me for hurting you, Billy." Laney looked into his blue eyes and saw them soften as she spoke. "I was afraid you'd talk me into staying so I didn't give you the chance. And Dane swept me off my feet promising me everything would be so much better."

"So what happened between you and your ex-husband?"

Laney stiffened. She looked at the ground and blew out a breath. "I guess I asked for that one."

"I don't want to make you uncomfortable, but I would like to understand where you're coming from." Billy gave her hand a squeeze.

Laney swallowed. "Dane adored me. He treated me like a queen, right up until I got pregnant. It was like he didn't want to share my attention with Oliver and he resented him for needing me. I kept hoping things would change once Oliver got a little older, but by the time I figured out who I really married, I felt trapped."

"I'm sorry." Billy frowned and he looked out the window as if seeing something else besides the trees swaying in the breeze. "How could anyone not fall for Oliver?"

"It wasn't just that," Laney said. "I didn't realize until after we were apart, but Dane only wanted me to act a certain way, to be interested in the same things as him. I didn't know him and he didn't know me. The problem was that I wanted to know him, but he didn't feel the same way about me." Laney felt a surge of emotion rising up her throat and did her best to swallow it back down. A few tears still leaked from the corner of her eyes.

Billy was quiet for a moment, probably digesting all that she'd unloaded. He looked at her, his eyes gentle and he touched the tear that had trickled down her cheek. "I'm sorry that you had to go through that. I'm sad that you had to be with someone who couldn't see you—how perfect you are because you're Laney."

Laney put her hand over his and gave him a half-smile. "You always knew who I was, even if I didn't."

Billy stepped forward and pulled her into his arms. "I still know you, even though you drive my heart crazy."

The words soaked in to Laney and she closed her eyes, loving the feel of Billy's arms around her. What did he mean when he said she drove his heart crazy? Did he still have feelings for her that extended beyond friendship? Laney wasn't sure if she should let herself hope, but she definitely wouldn't reject the idea of spending more time with Billy.

"A lot of things have changed for both of us, but I'm glad that some things haven't." Billy kissed the top of her head and then he released his hold on her. "I guess we'd better get this jail cell built."

Laney grabbed the paint can and started shaking it. "I'm ready." She smiled at Billy and noticed that he didn't look away. Maybe apologizing had rebuilt the bridge that she had destroyed so long ago—or at least started them on that path. She pretended to examine the spray paint closely, still feeling Billy's eyes on her.

CHAPTER 15

On Sunday Billy spent a few extra minutes getting ready for church. He told himself that it wasn't because he thought Laney might be there with her family, but the truth was apparent when he looked in the mirror. He couldn't stop grinning every time he thought about how Laney had apologized and a huge weight had been lifted from his shoulders. For the first time since he'd seen Laney in Echo Ridge it felt more like the old days. He knew it was dangerous to hope but a part of him wondered if there might be a chance for them to explore what they had lost so long ago.

Pastor Louis greeted Billy with a twinkle in his eye. "It's nice to see you here today."

"I'm looking forward to your sermon, Pastor."

Pastor Louis clapped him on the back. "I think you might find it interesting."

Billy walked through the chapel wondering what the topic might be and what Pastor Louis thought he knew about Billy's life that would make his sermon interesting today. Billy always enjoyed the sermons, although sometimes he didn't listen as intently as he should. He'd have to pay attention today.

Billy sat on the edge of the fourth row and tried to keep himself from looking around the chapel every thirty seconds to see if Laney had arrived. Finally, at five minutes to ten he caught sight of Laney tugging Oliver's hand as they walked toward the front of the chapel. Laney wore a pink and yellow flowered sundress and Oliver tugged on his grey and blue striped tie. There was room on Billy's pew for them to sit next to him but it looked like Laney might be heading toward the front. He'd watched the rest of the Richins family come in but then Susie Gibson had sat next to them and the bench looked a little crowded now. Billy straightened and lifted a hand and a wave. When Laney saw him her face lit up and she changed direction. By the time she reached his pew Billy's heart was pounding.

"Did you save us a seat?" Laney asked.

"I saved one for Oliver but it looks like there's room for you to," Billy replied.

Oliver grinned. "Mom, he saved me a seat."

"That's perfect, sweetie. Go ahead and sit down." Laney winked at Billy and his heart thumped harder.

Oliver sat next to Billy and Laney sat on the edge of the pew. Billy would have liked it if she had sat right next to him but maybe it was for the best because his heart was about ready to beat out of his chest having her on the same row. Billy was grateful that Kelli and her family weren't at church today because he would never be able to endure the teasing she would give him if she found him sitting beside Laney.

"You look beautiful," Billy leaned over Oliver and whispered to Laney.

"Thank you," she whispered back.

The opening hymn started and Billy forced himself to concentrate on the words instead of his nearness to Laney. Billy had to bite the inside of his cheek when Pastor Louis introduced the topic of his sermon for the day on The Prodigal Son. He glanced at Laney and she smiled at him unaware of the connection that Pastor Louis had made. How did the pastor always seem to know what was going on in his parishioner's lives? Billy often wondered if he had some sort of spy network set up. Billy leaned back against the pew and listened to one of his favorite parables from the Bible. Both he and Laney had left Echo Ridge and returned after several years. Laney had left with feelings similar to the prodigal son and now she'd returned and asked for forgiveness. He frowned, gnawing on his bottom lip.

He'd also left Echo Ridge and returned home, so who was the prodigal son, Laney or Billy?

Billy listened to the sermon and watched Laney help Oliver quietly color as Pastor Louis spoke of the return of the prodigal son and the joyful reunion and celebration on his behalf. Even though he'd turned his back on his family, his father welcomed him with enthusiasm. Billy understood the deeper meaning of the parable was forgiveness.

"We should never trap someone in their past sins and mistakes," Pastor Louis said in his melodic voice. "Instead, we should believe in the best. Believe that people can change, that we can change and become more like our Savior."

Although he spoke those words quietly, they pierced Billy's soul. The words he'd spoken to Laney were true—they were kids when they'd both made promises they couldn't keep. It was time to let that part of the past go and look to the future.

About halfway through the sermon Oliver got a little fidgety so Billy asked if he could help him color. Oliver gladly handed over a blue and green crayon and Billy helped him color in the edges of a dragon's wings. When they finished coloring the picture, Oliver leaned into his mother. Billy put his arm along the back of the pew resting his fingertips on Laney's shoulder. She turned to him and mouthed, *Thank you.* Billy nodded and forced himself to concentrate on the rest of the sermon. But Laney's soft skin under his fingertips proved to be quite the distraction. It seemed everyone in Echo Ridge was rooting for Billy and Laney to get together but there was so much more involved now. Oliver, and a cranky ex-husband, and the matter of how much his heart should trust Laney even as it pounded when she looked at him with those dark brown eyes of hers.

Afterwards at the potluck dinner, Laney invited Billy to sit with the rest of her family. Laney and Oliver had brought lemon bars and her mother Josi had a slow cooker full of her famous pulled pork. Billy loaded up his plate and joined the Richins family feeling only a tad bit awkward. But after a few minutes of chatting with Josi and Charlie he felt like hardly any time had passed at all.

Evangeline Hyatt stopped by their table and gave Billy's arm a squeeze. "This sure is a fine young gentle-man," she said giving Laney a wink. "Have you told her the good news?"

Billy shook his head adamantly. "No, I wanted to wait until everything was official."

"Oops. I guess the cat's out of the bag now." Evangeline patted his shoulder. "I think you should share the good news. You've signed the papers."

Billy felt his cheeks turning bright red and his neck flushed with embarrassment. He swallowed and his eyes flicked to Laney and her parents. "I'm going buy the Hyatt property. I hope to move in next month."

"Really?" Josi clapped her hands. "That *is* wonderful news. Oh Evangeline, I bet you're so relieved."

"You couldn't have asked for a better guy to take over ownership of that place," Charlie said. "Billy is about as handy as they come. Or so I've heard."

Billy straightened his shoulders, pulling back with pride. "Thank you, sir. I'm a bit nervous about undertaking so much property but I've loved that place since I was a kid."

"I'll talk to you later," Evangeline said. "Good to see you all."

Laney grabbed hold of Billy's arm. "When were you going to tell me?"

Billy shrugged. "I wanted to make sure that it was actually a possibility. Evangeline worked out some details for me and I have to come up with a hefty down payment."

"You'll do it," Laney said. "I remember how you used to talk about that place, the old barn, when we were kids."

Billy swallowed back the worry because there was nothing to do now but make sure that he came up with the money for the loan. By the time the potluck was over, all of Echo Ridge would know who the new owner of the Hyatt Farm would soon be. After the potluck Billy walked Laney and Oliver to her car.

"Thanks again for saving us a seat," Laney said. "It was nice to have lunch with you too."

Billy rubbed the back of his neck, trying to hide the sudden jitters that he felt. "Hey, I was wondering if tomorrow you might be able to come by, you and Oliver, and we could finish up the brig?"

"I think that'd be great. I get off at four so we could have an early dinner and then meet at your shop at six, would that work?"

"That'd be great." Billy wanted to ask her over for dinner but he felt like that might be pushing it a bit far. Better to see how things went with the project. "I think we'll be able to finish everything up tomorrow and we can get it prepped to take to the high school later this week."

"I guess we'll see you tomorrow." She opened the door of her car.

"Hey Laney, wait." Billy covered her hand with his. "I was wondering, have you taken Oliver to see the waterfall up Parley's Canyon since you've been back?"

Laney's features softened. "The waterfall. I almost forgot about it. I haven't been up there or thought about it in ages. Is there even water running this time of year?"

"Yep, the snowpack was high this past winter and I

heard it's still running fairly steady. Do you and Oliver want to drive up and see it later this afternoon?"

Laney grinned. "Are you asking us out on a date?"

"I guess so. Are you saying yes?"

Laney's smiled widened and she leaned forward on her tiptoes. "Yes."

Billy found himself matching her grin. "How about I pick you up at four?"

"Sounds like a plan."

Billy hardly remembered driving home, but when he got there he was still smiling. He had blurted out the invitation before he had time to talk himself out of it. And now he was taking Laney and her son to see the waterfall. The same waterfall where he and Laney had shared their first kiss. Billy groaned. It was like his subconscious was taking over. Laney probably had remembered the same thing which might make things a tad awkward. He decided not to dwell on that, instead he'd focus on remembering the genuine smile that had lit up Laney's face.

Billy took a Sunday afternoon nap and he dreamed about walking behind the barn with Laney on the Hyatt property. When he awoke he was more excited than ever to see her and spend time with her again. He cut up a few apples, washed some grapes and threw in a bag of cookies and headed over to Laney's house, arriving just before four. Oliver was so excited he was nearly jumping up and down with each step towards Billy's pickup. They chatted as they drove up Parley's Way passing the Ruby Mountain Resort and noticing the beautiful foliage.

"We'll have to come again next month when the leaves change," Laney said.

Billy nodded. "I wouldn't miss it." He loved the way she was making plans to spend time with him. Billy did his best to include Oliver in the conversation, pointing out some of his favorite spots along the canyon including the huge blue spruce that had been there since he was a little kid. When they pulled off the road to hike to the waterfall, Billy helped Oliver out and he shouldered the backpack full of goodies.

"What's that?" Oliver asked.

"Hiking treats," Billy replied.

Laney laughed. "I remember your hiking treats. Chocolate, gummy bears, Pop Rocks. Billy has a sweet tooth," she said to her son.

"So does your mama." Billy put his arm around Laney and pulled her in close, tickling her side. "She's the one who brought all the sweet treats and insisted that there were never enough gummy bears."

Oliver watched them with a smile. "Do you like my mom?"

Billy hesitated for a second. He glanced at Laney who was watching him with an arched eyebrow, as if daring him to tell the truth. "Your mom and I have been best friends since we were about your age."

"Really?" Oliver scrunched up his nose. "That's weird. All of my friends are boys."

Everyone laughed and Billy led the way as they hiked up the trail to the waterfall. The trail switched back in a few places but the incline was gradual, perfect for Oliver's short legs and for a leisurely walk on the late afternoon hike. Thankfully the heatwave had broken and the temperatures in the mountains were cooler. The trail forked and Billy led them to the base of the waterfall. As they approached, a fine mist tickled their skin.

Laney gasped. "I'd forgotten how beautiful it is." She pulled Oliver closer. "Look up there, Buddy. When you get older we'll hike to the top."

She looked over the top of Oliver's head and gave Billy a warning look. He knew exactly what she was remembering. Billy had hiked up to the top and jumped off into the pool below more times than he could count. She didn't want him mentioning that to her five-year-old son and giving him any ideas. Billy watched Laney as she pointed out the rocks and the trees surrounding the waterfall. Strands of her hair had come loose from her ponytail and they curled around her face. She was beautiful in an unassuming way. She only wore a bit of mascara and Billy wasn't sure if she even had lipstick on but she looked more beautiful than he remembered.

Laney must have felt him watching her because she turned toward him. She smiled at him and Billy nodded, admitting he'd been caught staring at her. He walked toward her and Oliver. "It's been a long time since I've been up here."

"I'm glad you thought of this," Laney said. "We made some good memories here."

"I wondered if you would remember."

"My first kiss?" Laney said softly. "Of course. A girl never forgets her first kiss."

Billy's eyes flicked to her lips, remembering that day with more clarity than he wanted to admit. He took in a breath, sucking in courage from the mountains around him to say what was on his mind. "Laney I'd like to see more of you. I don't want to scare you away, but I feel like we need to give this a chance." He reached out his hand and interlaced his fingers with hers.

Laney squeezed his hand and stepped closer. "I agree. It scares me a little, but Oliver and I have already been on our own for almost a year."

Billy felt heat rush through him at Laney's nearness. She hadn't shrunk from his suggestion, she'd agreed and come closer to him. "I didn't realize it had been that long," Billy said.

Laney nodded. "I separated from Dane, but it took a while before the divorce was final and then we decided to move here. It turned out to be the best choice for us."

"That reminds me. I ran into Dane last week?"

"You did?" Laney's eyes widened. "Was it Friday?"

Billy nodded. "I didn't mention it at first because I wasn't sure what to make of him. I took a lunch break and when I came out he was standing by my truck. He told me to stay away from his wife."

Laney growled. "What an idiot. He was waiting for me when I got off work that night." She looked over at Oliver. He was crouched next to the base of the waterfall laughing as a spray tickled his face. The roar of the water hid their conversation. "The thing that drives me crazy is he came to talk to me and didn't even ask about our son."

"Does he have visitation rights?"

"No, he didn't want them." Laney folded her arms. "And I thank my lucky stars that he signed away those rights before he changed his mind. Although I doubt he will ever change his mind."

"So why did he come by? What does he expect to get from you? It's not like you're going to leave Oliver."

Laney shrugged. "I understand him less now than when I was married to him. There's really no reason for me to see him. I told him to leave. He mentioned you, but I thought he was just saying stuff. I can't believe he came to talk to you."

"You'll let me know if he gives you any trouble won't you?"

Laney turned to him. "I will. Thanks, Billy. I don't think he would ever try to hurt me but he's definitely threatened some strange things in the past."

"What I can't figure out is how he even knew where to find me. Was he just driving around Echo Ridge until he saw my pickup?"

Laney narrowed her eyes. "That is something to think about. He said he looked up your construction company. He was always the jealous type and he knew all about you because every memory I have of home had you in it. I finally stopped talking about my past because I could see how it bothered him. I think that's why I had forgotten a lot of the good things. Since moving back here, so much is coming back—so many memories that I love."

Billy suddenly felt protective of Laney and Oliver. The little boy was playing with rocks a few feet from the water's edge. Billy stepped closer to Laney, wrapping his arms around her. Laney relaxed against him and Billy pressed his cheek against hers. "Let me know if there's anything I can do for you, okay?"

Laney turned and her lips were a breath away from him. She put her hand on his cheek. "I will," she murmured.

Billy looked at her mouth, and then into her eyes trying to gauge her feelings. Laney's face was open, welcoming his closeness. He closed the gap between them, kissing her softly, hesitating to see if she would return the kiss. Laney leaned in closer, kissing him back. She wrapped her arms around his neck. Billy pulled her closer, kissing her mouth and feeling a thrill at the soft sigh that escaped her lips.

The powerful sound of the waterfall surged around them and for a moment Billy felt like they had stepped back in time—two teenagers holding each other close, kissing underneath the spray of the waterfall with their whole lives in front of them. But this didn't feel like the kisses they'd shared back then. This kiss overpowered him, with everything he'd loved about Laney so long ago. He tasted her sweetness, every vibrant moment he'd spent with her and he knew it wasn't enough. So much had changed since then and somehow they'd returned to the same spot. Billy kissed Laney again, holding her closer.

"Mommy? What you doing?" Oliver's little voice broke the silence.

Laney gasped and stepped away from Billy, but he held on to her waist. "I'm kissing your mommy because she's the most beautiful woman I know and I like her a lot," Billy replied before Laney could answer.

"And I'm kissing Billy because I like him a lot." Laney crouched near Oliver and kissed him on the cheek. "But don't tell Billy that I like you best of all."

Oliver grinned and whispered, "I won't."

Billy laughed and when Laney stood next to him, her dark brown eyes shining, he felt his heart surge with love. It was love he felt for Laney and he wondered if he'd ever stopped loving her or if Laney had held on to his heart from the first kiss they shared when they were fifteen. The way Laney was looking at him, he thought there was a good chance that she was considering the same things.

When Laney went to work practically floating on air Monday morning, it only took two minutes for Paisley to get the story out of her.

"You kissed him?"

"He kissed me. I kissed him. He kissed me again. Yes, we kissed and it was amazing." Laney lifted up on her tiptoes.

Paisley shook her head. "I knew you had it bad for that boy."

"You're right, I did have it bad for that boy when I was a teenager, but he's not a boy anymore." Laney sighed remembering kissing Billy the man. "I have to say it was more than I expected. And I'd do it again in a heartbeat."

Paisley clicked her tongue. "I'd better have you working late then. To keep you out of trouble."

"Oliver and I are going over to his place tonight to finish up the brig."

"Just don't let things move too fast," Paisley cautioned.

"Don't worry," Laney replied. "I'm listening to my heart *and* my head this time."

Laney texted Billy before she left work and asked if she could pick up some sandwiches from Fay's Cafe to bring to his shop so they could eat dinner together.

Her phone chimed with Billy's response: *Sounds perfect!*

Laney loved the way her stomach flipped when he answered right away and she counted down the minutes until she would see him next. Oliver was also excited to see his friend Billy and have a chance to work with his tools. Laney picked up the sandwiches and they made it to Billy's shop at five.

Billy looked good wearing carpenter jeans and a bright green t-shirt. He greeted her with a peck on the cheek. "It's good to see you."

"You too. I've been looking forward to this all day."

Oliver stepped forward and tugged on Billy's hand. "Do you have any more Berenstain Bear books?"

"You know I actually do have a whole collection of them," Billy replied. He smiled at Laney and ruffled the top of Oliver's head. "Maybe we could check them out sometime."

"You mean at the library?" Oliver asked

"No at my house."

"You mean you don't live here?" Oliver looked around the shop and Laney saw the moment he recognized that there wasn't a bed, just tools and equipment.

"This is just where Billy works," Laney said.

"Yep, I have a house, but we're going to eat over on this table tonight," Billy replied. "Does that sound like fun?"

"Yes! I get my own sandwich." Oliver followed Billy to a work table covered with a plastic tablecloth.

They enjoyed a quick meal with Oliver dominating the conversation with stories from kindergarten. Billy asked Oliver lots of questions and as Laney watched them interact, she fell a little bit more in love with Billy Redford.

Billy wadded up his sandwich wrapper. "I guess we'd better get busy before it gets too late."

"Yes, I'm excited to see the finished project," Laney said.

"I think I have this fastened together the right way." Billy pointed to the corner where Laney saw the black spray painted crib against the wall. She thought of the funny expression on the clerk's face and started laughing again so hard that she snorted.

"Did you just snort?" Billy started laughing and then

Laney laughed harder. Oliver soon joined the melee and they were all laughing. It felt good.

Billy tugged on Laney's ponytail lightly. "So I was hoping you would help me get this side put together tonight." He picked up a drill and a handful of screws.

"Whatever you say, boss." Laney traced her fingers along the back of his neck until he shivered.

Billy stepped away from Laney, pretending her touch hadn't affected him. "This is for you." Billy handed Oliver a screwdriver and a piece of wood with several screws inserted halfway into the plank. "I wanted to know if you could tighten these for me."

Oliver grinned. "I'll try my best."

Laney watched Oliver sit down in the sawdust-covered floor and immediately start working on tightening the screws that Billy had prepared for him. "That was really nice of you to think of him."

"I remember being his age," Billy said. "I always wanted to help out and the tools were too big for my little hands."

Laney balanced the sheet of plywood while Billy pre-drilled holes for the framework. "Tell me more about the Hyatt place. I can't believe you were keeping that a secret from me."

"I can't believe Evangeline told everybody at the potluck. I might as well have taken out an ad in the paper," Billy said.

"She looked really happy about it. My mom told me afterwards that Evangeline had been worrying herself sick when Winston was on the downhill slope. She didn't know what to do with the property. I think it's wonderful that you'll be able to have your dream come true and help her at the same time."

Billy's mouth twitched and Laney wondered what worries he had on his mind. "Why aren't you more excited about it?"

"I'm just worried is all. I drained my savings to start my business and things have been going well but not well enough that I can afford to shell out ten grand for a down payment when I wasn't even looking to buy a house."

"Oh, I didn't realize. That probably is tricky."

Billy shook his head. "I know I need to have more faith. Evangeline has worked this out so that I'll rent-to-own the property. I'll have a lower payment at first and have a chance to work and fix up things on the farm which I'll get credit for. It's just a really big step, one that I wasn't anticipating taking so soon."

Laney put her hand over his. "I think that happens a lot in life. We aren't ready to climb the next hill or take the turn that looks wrong or move to a new place, return to our hometown. Having faith has helped but I'm still worried too."

Billy set the drill down. "I really am excited about the

property. As soon as my mom told me it was up for sale I went for a drive and took a look at it. I even wrote down the number to the realtor. I didn't end up calling him because I figured it was out of my budget—and then to have it fall in my lap. It almost seems too good to be true."

"It probably is too good to be true. It will be a lot of work. It will be a big risk for you, but you should definitely go for it. If anybody can make it work, you can."

"Thanks, Laney. That means a lot to me."

"I'd like to ride out with you sometime and see the property. Maybe I'll have a few ideas of what you need to do to fix it up. Remember how we used to talk about that when we were kids?"

"I'm starting to think there wasn't much we didn't talk about as kids." Billy winked.

"Look Billy! I got this screw all the way in!" Oliver exclaimed. He held up the piece of wood. He might have turned the screw about three rotations. Laney smiled.

"Good job," Billy said. "Now keep working on those other two and see if you can get them in a little bit farther."

Oliver beamed at Billy and gripped the screwdriver tighter. Laney reached up on her toes and kissed Billy lightly on the lips.

"What was that for?" Billy asked.

"Nothing. You're just being you and I think you're pretty handsome and wonderful."

The tips of Billy's ears turned pink and he glanced over to where Oliver was playing with the piece of wood. "Thank you," he murmured. "I guess we'd better finish this up."

Billy had just drilled the last hole on the sheet of plywood when they heard something clatter to the floor. Laney looked across the room and saw Oliver on top of the work table with the saw in his hand. She screamed and Billy took off running across the room. Oliver jumped when Laney screamed and tilted backwards almost falling off the table.

"Put that down, Oliver. You're going to get hurt!" Billy snatched him off the top of the table. "What were you thinking?"

Oliver's lip trembled. "I was just trying to work hard."

Laney examined the work table and gasped when she saw two pieces of an electric cord sawed in half. "Oliver, what did you do?"

Billy's eyes flicked to where Laney was studying the cord. "Oh no, he didn't."

"I was fixing things." Oliver's voice was small.

Billy picked up two ends of the cord and then he picked up the saw and examined the teeth that had bits of black casing stuck in them.

"What does that go to?" Laney asked.

"My skill saw," Billy answered as he dropped the pieces of cord onto the table. "I have a big job tomorrow I'm supposed to be using this on. I'll have to borrow one from somebody else.

"Oh no. Billy I'm so sorry. I should have been watching him better." She was horrified that Oliver could have been electrocuted.

Billy looked down at the ground. "It's okay. I think we were both pretty distracted. You'd better go now. This is probably not the best place to be working with Oliver."

Laney felt sick to her stomach. Oliver was crying. She took his hand and turned to go. "I'm really sorry. I'll pay for it to be repaired. Just tell me what to do."

"I can fix it. It'll just take a while." Billy's voice was quiet. "I'll give Carter a call over at the Bed and Breakfast. I know he has a nice skill saw that will work."

Laney hurried out, too embarrassed to say anything else. When they got in the car, Oliver kept sniffling as they drove home. "It's okay, bud. You didn't mean to."

"Billy was mad at me. He yelled at me. I don't like him anymore."

Laney reached back and patted Oliver's knee. "Please don't say that. Billy wasn't mad at you. He was scared that you were going to get hurt. Mommy is mad at you because you climbed up on that table and I've told you a hundred times not to climb on things. Mommy was scared too. I don't want you to get hurt. Do you understand Oliver?"

"Yeah."

"When we get home we need to think about how you can apologize to Billy. Maybe we can make him a treat tomorrow."

Oliver sighed. "Okay."

The only good part about the incident was that they got home early so Oliver could go to bed on time. He didn't want to read the *Honey Hunt* and that made Laney feel bad. She didn't try to press the issue though. She just reminded Oliver that they would need to make things right because he broke Billy's tool. Then she kissed him goodnight.

Once Oliver was asleep, Laney took a glass of iced tea out onto the porch. She sat on the front porch steps and looked out at the sun sinking low on the horizon.

"I see you're still following your rituals."

Laney jolted, spilling iced tea on her capris. Dane stood on her front yard not ten feet away. "What are you doing here?" She set the iced tea down and stood slowly.

"I came by to see how you're doing." Dane walked forward as he spoke. "I'm guessing Oliver is asleep?"

A bitter taste crawled up the back of Laney's throat. Even the way Dane said Oliver's name hinted at contempt. "I want you to leave right now."

Dane kept walking forward. "Laney, I'm worried about you. I'm not here to upset you. I just want to make sure you have what you need—that Oliver has what he needs."

"Since when do you give a pig's eye about your son?" Laney gripped the railing, trying to hide the shaking in her hands.

Dane climbed the bottom step. "I've always cared about our son. You never understood what it was like for me even though I explained it a hundred times. I went to a boarding school. I was never around my parents. That was just how it was. And yet you expected me to be someone I wasn't."

Laney put her hand out. "Just stop. I'm not having this argument with you again. History doesn't define the future. We all have a choice. You made yours and I made mine. I would appreciate it if you would leave now."

Dane climbed the next step and reached toward her hand. Laney was frozen to the spot. She thought about screaming but she didn't want to wake up Oliver. And Dane had never hurt her. At least not physically.

"Don't look so scared, Laney. I'm not here to hurt you. I'm here to help you. I want you to think about what you're doing. You hated this town. You said it suffocated you. Why did you come back here? You think your only choice is to get back with Billy Redford?"

"I was young and stupid, obviously because I married you," Laney spat.

Dane took another step up until he was standing right next to Laney. "I think you're deluding yourself because you don't know where else to go. I'm here to tell you that if you want to come back I'll do better. I'll take those parenting classes you wanted and figure out how to be a father to Oliver."

Laney sucked in a breath. She'd never heard Dane promise anything even remotely close to what he was saying. What did he really want? Worry snaked up her spine. She didn't like how close Dane was to her, but they were standing on her front steps so she couldn't imagine that he would try anything.

"Before you throw your life away on that low-life Billy who will work himself into an early grave, you need to consider what's standing right in front of you." Dane leaned forward and kissed Laney, putting his arms around her and pulling her close to him.

Laney's eyes widened and she tried to pull back. She saw movement and looked behind Dane to see Billy standing on her front lawn. The look on his face was one of crushing betrayal. His eyes widened, he shook his head, and then he spun and walked to his truck.

Laney put her hands on Dane's chest and pushed him back so that he had to jump off the steps or risk falling. She ran after Billy. "Wait, Billy! Please wait."

Billy slammed the door of his truck and the engine roared to life. He couldn't hear Laney as she called after him. When she turned around, Dane was standing on the front step a smug look on his face. Laney pointed at him. "You will get off my property and never return or I'll call the police right now and get a restraining order."

Dane lifted up his hands. "No need. I'm leaving." He walked down the steps toward her and as he passed he called over his shoulder, "That was quite the kiss. Remember that and remember I can offer a lot more than Billy Redford can."

Laney clenched her fists, screaming inside as she sat down onto her front porch steps. She leaned her head forward, resting on her knees, as the tears poured out. Dane was just messing with her like he always did. Hopefully that would be the last of him since he got what he came for. Laney tried to call Billy but he didn't answer. She texted him, explaining that Dane had forced the kiss and that she didn't know what he was doing in Echo Ridge. When there was still no reply she went to bed, her eyes puffy and her heart tired.

Billy woke up Tuesday morning with a rock in his gut. No matter how hard he tried he couldn't get the image of Dane kissing Laney out of his mind. An internal argument ensued with one part of Billy believing that Laney hadn't wanted to kiss Dane just like her text had said and the other part wondering what game she was playing by coming back to Echo Ridge and having her ex-husband follow her.

He needed time to cool off so he didn't answer any of her calls or texts. He immersed himself in work and when he continued to ignore Laney, she stopped contacting him. He had a headache that pinched behind his eyes and he wasn't sure what to do. So instead of figuring it out, he focused on work. He finished up the platform for the photo backdrop, wondering how he would handle the awkwardness of the homecoming dance if Laney decided to show up.

Over the next few days Billy logged almost a week's worth of work catching up on several projects and getting ahead on others. Laney wasn't his only problem because every time he checked his bank account the numbers didn't add up to the ten thousand dollar down payment he needed by the end of the month. He took on extra jobs and considered taking a loan against his work truck for the remainder. He even went so far as to meet with the bank president. They went over the paperwork and he cautioned Billy about borrowing against his truck. He told him to try to see if he could borrow a few thousand dollars from his parents first. That didn't sit well with Billy because he prided himself on building up his business from scratch, not having to borrow money from anyone. But when the numbers continued to fall short Billy knew that he couldn't let this chance to purchase the Hyatt property pass by.

On Thursday he asked his mom and dad if he could stop by on his lunch break for a few minutes. Lee and Norma Redford greeted their son with a hug and a handshake. Billy wondered if they already knew what he was about to ask them so he decided to get it over with.

"Mom and Dad, I wanted to talk to you about my plans to purchase the Hyatt property."

"I think it's a wonderful idea, son." Lee said.

"How much do you need for the down payment?" Norma asked.

Billy chuckled. "You always were a mind reader, Mom. I have to put down ten thousand dollars."

"I thought it would be more than that," Lee said. "How many acres are there?"

"Six acres and Evangeline wants me to have the property so she worked out a way that I can rent to own but I have to put the ten grand down to show my commitment."

Lee nodded. "I see, and the bank probably doesn't want to loan the small amount on top of the mortgage that you'll be applying for in the next couple years."

"That's right. I'm worried about draining my emergency savings account because everything has been working smoothly right now so that I can pay my crew and keep up with supplies but if somebody is late it could put me in a hard position."

"We'll loan you the money," Lee said.

"I hate to ask. Part of me wonders if this is a bad idea," Billy said. "Who do I think I am buying this huge property and house and I don't even have a girlfriend?"

"Oh?" Norma grabbed hold of his arm. "What have you done? I thought you and Laney were seeing each other."

Billy shook his head. "We've been working on this backdrop for the homecoming dance and it's been a lot of fun. But the other night her little boy cut through the cord on my skill saw and I got upset. They left and when I went by her house to apologize she was out on her front porch kissing her ex-husband."

Norma gasped. Lee shook his head. "Are you sure you know what you were actually seeing?"

Billy folded his arms and frowned. "What do you mean?"

"Well, was she kissing him or was he kissing her? I've heard about him from Laney's father. He's a low life who abandoned his own child. He's a smooth talker and he thinks he can always get what he wants."

"Have you talked to Laney about it?" Norma asked.

Billy's shoulders slumped. "I couldn't. I've been ignoring her."

"Well that will sure clear up a lot of things," Lee said.

"Billy, go talk to her, please." Norma squeezed Billy's forearm. "If there's any chance that she wasn't kissing him then what was happening? You need to be there to support her. Wouldn't you want her to give you the same opportunity if the tables were turned?"

Billy sighed, letting his arms drop to his sides. "It's not just that. I'm feeling overwhelmed. I feel like everyone in Echo Ridge is pushing us together but maybe it's not the right thing. It wasn't the right thing before and I ended up getting my heart broken."

"Just because things didn't turn out exactly how you

envisioned them doesn't necessarily mean it wasn't the right thing before," Norma said. "You and Laney needed experience. You needed to grow up. Do you think you would have ever started your own construction company if you hadn't gone out and worked with some of those big companies?"

Billy looked at the floor, letting his mother's words sink in.

"Do you still love her after all these years?" Lee asked, his voice soft.

Billy lifted his head to look at his parents. "I'm afraid to say it but I think I do. I thought I was over her. I was angry at her when she first showed up but then she found a way to get under my skin again."

Lee chuckled. "The right woman has a way of doing that."

"Love is always scary. It's never going to be exactly how we think it should but that's what makes it all worth it." Norma patted his hand. "Don't let the best thing you could ever have get away because you're scared."

"Maybe there's a reason Evangeline wanted you to have this property," Lee said. "There may be a lot more in your future than you know. Don't worry about that down payment."

"Dad, I'll pay you back as soon as I can," Billy replied.

Lee shook his head and smiled. "Your mother and I have a secret that we made Kelli keep from you."

Norma grinned and put her arm around Lee. "We have a special savings account with the down payment for your first home. When Kelli and Greg bought their first home we gave them their down payment."

Billy's eyes widened. "Wow, that's—I had no idea. That's really great."

"We think so too," Lee said. "When we started the fund we figured it would happen when you're married and had a family and ready to move into your family home but it looks like things for you are moving a little faster. We'll cover the full down payment for the Hyatt property and we don't expect anything in return."

Billy's jaw dropped. He'd been raised in a modest home with a principle of frugality that taught him to work hard and be grateful for what he had. He'd known no extravagances and even after he and Kelli left home, his parents continued to be careful spenders. "But how can you—"

"It's wonderful when you can help your children find a little piece of happiness." Norma's eyes twinkled. "We know how much that property means to you, and Evangeline knew that no one else could restore it to the state it should be in. It's a perfect place to raise a family."

Billy could hardly believe his ears. All his life his parents had taught him to work hard, save his money, and make his own way. He and Kelli had grown up not asking for much, instead they would get odd jobs when they needed money to buy something. He felt like he'd just won the lottery. Billy hugged his mom and dad. "Thanks. This really means a lot to me. I've been working really hard and every time I tried to talk myself out of buying this property I just couldn't. It feels like the right thing to do."

"That's because it is," Lee said.

"Now go talk to Laney," Norma commanded.

"I'll do that." Billy hugged his parents again and hurried out to his truck. Suddenly the day looked a lot brighter.

*L*aney couldn't remember the last time she'd had such a bad week. Homecoming week in Echo Ridge was notoriously busy and the flower shop had so many orders that Paisley had to call a temp agency to send over a worker to help them keep up with everything. But that wasn't the part that made her week horrible. Staying busy was the only thing that kept her from agonizing over what to do about Billy Redford.

Dane had left a note on her front door Tuesday morning telling her that he was planning to move to Echo Ridge to be the father that Oliver needed. Her first thoughts were to contact a lawyer, but then she remembered all the times in the past when Dane would stir up trouble just for fun. She decided to survive the week and if Dane came around again, she'd just call the police. Laney felt sick to her stomach every time she thought of her slimy ex-husband. She hated not knowing what game he was trying to play. She had confided her worries to her parents, but insisted that Oliver be sheltered from any knowledge of the situation. Her father was ready to drive around the town to hunt Dane, but luckily Mom was able to calm her husband down.

It was seven o'clock by the time Laney got off work on Thursday and her feet and back ached. Poor Oliver had been shuffled around to every family member who could take him. At least he seemed happy about the time he'd spent at his grandparents' and cousins' homes.

Laney shouldered her purse which felt like she was carrying boxes of nails. She walked quickly to her car, eager to get this day over with and have time to put her feet up that night. There was a dark SUV parked next to her car and as she walked around she saw Dane leaning against her door. She stopped and pulled her cell phone out of her purse. "You have thirty seconds to get away from my vehicle or I'm calling the police," Laney said, fear prickling the back of her neck.

Dane narrowed his eyes. "You're not going to call the police because I'm not doing anything wrong. This is public property. I'm standing in the middle of a parking lot and you happened to walk up and start talking to me." Dane flipped his sunglasses up on his head and sneered. "I thought it would be rude to ignore you."

Laney shook her head. "I'm not playing any games here. I want you gone. Gone from this town."

"I don't remember seeing anything in our divorce decree that stated I couldn't live in the same town as my son."

Laney swallowed the acid in the back of her throat as his implications hit her. "Dane, what do you want?"

He took a step forward and Laney took a step back, gripping her cell phone and trying to decide if he she should just call 911.

"I want you. I told you that. I remember you saying that I always get what I want, and I want you." He winked. Dane took another step toward her.

"I warned you." Laney held up her phone, her hand shaking, and then she flipped the screen towards her and started dialing. She heard the asphalt crunch beneath Dane's feet and he grabbed the phone out of her hands before she had a chance to react.

"Stop!" Laney screamed. Her voice rang in her ears, a hollow sound filled with terror. She didn't know what Dane was capable of, and the quietness of the parking lot pressed in on her.

"I'm not going to hurt you. I just want to talk to you for a minute."

Dane was a terrible husband and father. He was manipulative and emotionally abusive but Laney had never been physically afraid of him before that moment.

The look on his face was dangerous. She opened up her mouth to scream again but she heard the sound of a pickup driving up right behind her. Dane's eyes widened and Laney looked behind her to see Billy jump out of his truck. Relief flooded her chest and she sucked in a shaky breath.

"Is he bothering you?" Billy asked as he strode to Laney's side and put a hand on her back.

"He took my phone and he's threatening me." Laney pointed at Dane. With Billy beside her, Laney felt a burst of courage. "Give me the phone."

Dane held up his hands innocently and then handed Laney her phone. "I was just making polite conversation. I don't know what the problem is." He shrugged. "I thought it'd be courteous to let Laney know I'll be moving to Echo Ridge so that I can be close to our son."

Billy looked at Laney. "Is this true?"

Dane stepped forward and grabbed Laney's arm jerking her forward. "I want you to stay away from him. He has no claim to you." Dane glared at Billy. "Stay away from my wife."

Laney jerked her arm back. "Let go of me!"

Billy pulled his arm back and punched Dane in the face. "She's not your wife—you got a divorce, remember? She's my girlfriend. You're not moving back to this town. You're leaving."

Dane held his nose, blood spurting around his fingers. "I'll sue you. You won't see the end of me."

Billy grabbed Dane by the front of his collar. "You are *not* going to sue me. You won't contact Laney again. You'll leave this town and never come back. Is that clear?" He gave Dane a shake and pushed him backwards against the SUV. "I did a little homework. I know things about you that Laney never did. I know that your business has gone belly-up and you're here hunting around trying to figure out a way to keep the state from garnishing your wages."

Dane gasped and wiped blood across his sleeve. "You don't know what you're talking about." He spat. "You don't even know who I am."

"You're right I didn't know much about you, but luckily Laney's father did know a lot about his former son-in-law and he was more than happy to help me do a little research. I took the liberty of making a few phone calls to alert an investigator as to your whereabouts."

Dane stepped back slowly. "It's not true." He turned to Laney. "Don't believe him. I'll leave. I won't bother you anymore."

The words fell on Laney like sheets of glass, shredding everything she thought she knew about her ex-husband, but with each painful slash, Laney felt the truth of Billy's revelations. In that moment, Laney was more than grateful that Oliver wasn't there to witness the scene, and that he didn't have contact with his horrible father. She lifted her chin, her chest swelling with anger. "I've known Billy for a long time and I've never known him to lie to me or anyone. He's telling the truth. And I'm telling the truth when I say I'll be filing a restraining order against you."

Dane swore and scrambled around the SUV, hopped in the driver's seat, and sped away.

Billy pulled Laney close to him, wrapping his arms around her. "Are you okay?"

Her hands trembled as her body shook with adrenaline. "I knew Dane was no good but I didn't know his business was in trouble."

"I'm worried about you. I hope that he won't come back around here."

Laney shook her head. "I'm not worried anymore. Dane is a coward. He won't come back. Thanks to you."

"And your dad. Your parents care about you so much. They want you to be happy."

Laney swallowed. "I am happy here—I mean I was until Dane came back and ruined everything."

"He didn't ruin anything." Billy stepped back, putting his hands on her arms. "I meant what I said Laney, I want you to be my girlfriend. I want to spend more time with you and Oliver. I was coming over here tonight because I already stopped by your house and found that you were still at work. I'm so sorry about how I acted."

"It's been a terrible week," Laney said, trying her best to keep the emotion from cracking her voice.

"Well, I want to do my best to help it end well. Come here." Billy led her to his truck where the door still hung wide open. On the seat was a gift sack. "This is for you and I have something for Oliver too, but I'd really like to give it to him if that's okay."

Laney swallowed back tears. Everything about Billy was so different from Dane. "You didn't have to get me a gift."

"I wanted to because I felt bad about how things went Monday night. When I came over to your house to apologize, Dane was there and I kind of exploded."

"I promise that didn't mean anything. I tried to tell you."

"I know." Billy touched her cheek. "And I did a horrible job at listening. I needed some time to cool off and think things through. Too many big decisions in my life right now." He nudged the gift sack. "Go on, open it."

Laney pulled back the silver and purple tissue paper to see cute black and white polka dot fabric with ruffles inside. "What's this?" She pulled it out and then smiled. "It's an apron."

"Not just any apron. Look at all those pockets," Billy pointed out. "I thought it might help you at work."

Laney held the apron to her chest. Billy must have noticed the ragged-looking apron that she wore when she worked on flowers in the shop. The pattern was mostly splatters and stains and all ragged edges. "Thank you. This is so thoughtful."

"I'm glad you like it." Billy tilted his head toward his pickup. "What do you think about delivering Oliver's gift?"

"He's over at my parents' house," Laney replied. "Would you like to come with me to get him?"

"I'd love to. Let me help you to your car first."

When she was safely tucked in her car, he got back in his pickup and followed her over to her parents' house. He carried a box up the front steps and Laney opened the door to let him in.

"Knock knock. We're here," Laney called. "If there's a little boy named Oliver here I think there's a special visitor for him."

She heard a squeal and Oliver skidded around the corner, bumped into her legs and then shouted, "It's Billy."

Billy knelt down, setting the box on the floor. "I brought you something because I wanted to tell you I'm sorry I got mad at you for cutting up the cord in my shop."

Oliver looked down at the floor. "I'm really sorry I broke your tools."

"That's okay." Billy patted Oliver's shoulder. "We both learned a lesson. I got something to help us out in the future. You want to open up this box and see what it is?"

Oliver approached the box and pulled the flaps back. "It's a tool box. My own tool box!" He cried out and jumped up and down. He lifted out a shiny red toolbox perfect for a five-year-old. Laney watched as Billy showed him the different compartments and her heart thrummed to a new, happy tune. How could she be so lucky to have Billy come back into her life and restore her belief that there were men in her world who make wonderful fathers? God was definitely smiling on her.

Oliver scampered off to show his grandparents his new tool box and Billy stood up brushing off his knees. Laney hugged him and kissed his cheek. "Thank you."

"You're welcome." He turned and kissed her lightly on the lips.

Laney felt a thrill down to her pinky toes. "So I was wondering, would you like to take me to the homecoming dance?"

"Hey, I was about to ask you the same thing." Billy nuzzled her neck. "We're supposed to be there to set everything up Saturday morning at ten."

"I can't think of anything I'd rather do." Laney giggled at the soft sandpaper feel of his face against hers.

"It's a date then," Billy murmured, and covered her mouth with another kiss.

CHAPTER 19

The backdrop was the perfect photo op for the pirate-themed homecoming dance. It was sturdy enough to stand up to groups of high school kids banging against the makeshift bars and all of the foliage Paisley had brought in gave it a tropical feel. Laney's parents stopped by with Oliver to see the setup and they insisted on getting a picture of Billy, Laney, and Oliver together.

"This town is lucky to have your talents," Josi said. "Both of you."

Billy grinned and pulled Laney next to his side. "I couldn't have done it without Miss Bossypants."

Laney pinched his side and he yelped. "See what I mean?"

"Thanks for bringing Oliver," Laney said, ignoring Billy's fake protests. "I can take him home from here."

"Stay and dance," Josi urged. "How many times do you get a second chance to go to your homecoming dance?"

Billy raised an eyebrow and tilted his head, inviting Laney to stay. "She makes a good point." He held his hand out. "Wanna dance with me?"

"Actually, I do." She kissed Oliver's cheek. "Be good for Grandma and Grandpa."

"I will. Grandpa's going to play Yahtzee with me." He waved and followed Josi and Charlie out of the gym.

"Your parents are great," Billy said.

"I know." Laney let him lead her to the middle of the dance floor.

Billy twirled Laney and then pulled her in close. He reached up and loosened his tie. "Ah, that's better. I can't believe you made me wear this getup."

Laney laughed and put her head against his shoulder. When she didn't stop laughing, Billy nuzzled her with his cheek. "What's so funny?"

"You." Laney touched his cheek. "Right there. You're just like Oliver, tugging at your tie and complaining about dressing up."

"So you're saying I'm just like your five-year-old son?"

Laney nodded. "Yep, that's what I'm saying, Red."

Billy grinned. "I like it when you call me Red."

"Why? Everybody called you Red in high school."

Billy shook his head. "Nobody said it like you did. The way your 'R' rolls with that edge. My name sounds different coming from your lips."

Laney looked at his lips and then back to his eyes. "Well, Red, I like a lot of things about you too."

"Like what?"

"Like the way you care about me and notice little things, like my ratty apron at the flower shop that needed replacing."

"I'm glad you liked that, but it was just an apron."

"No, it wasn't just an apron. It was something that took some thought, like the toolbox you got for Oliver. You noticed me, us, and it means a lot."

Billy hummed along to the music playing as they danced in the midst of high school kids. It seemed so long ago that Laney was an innocent senior at Echo Ridge High, dancing with Billy with a sketch of their whole life planned out for them. It hadn't turned out anything like that sketch but somehow she had ended up back in his arms.

"Remember the treehouse?" Billy nuzzled her neck.

Laney nodded. "I remember."

"Well, I want to build you something better than a treehouse. I want to build a life with you so that every day we can have that excitement and anticipation of building something on our own. Will you give me a second chance?"

"I think that sounds like a brilliant idea." Laney smiled and her eyes filled with tears. She hugged him, feeling the breath catch in her chest. Billy was offering her a second chance at the life she'd always wanted. It took her leaving Echo Ridge to discover that her dreams were waiting for her right in her hometown. "And Billy?" Laney kissed him and then went up on her tiptoes and whispered in his ear. "If you want to build something for us, I think I have an extra box of nails."

The End

Continue reading for a sneak peek of the 5th book in the bestselling Echo Ridge Romance series! *Her Guy Next Door Fake Fiancé*

Grandma Suzy's Famous Chicken Salad

8 chicken breasts cooked, chopped
1 small can water chestnuts
1 small can crushed pineapple
¼ cup chopped onion
¼ cup celery, chopped
½ cup red grapes, sliced
1 cup sour cream
1 cup mayonnaise
Salt and pepper to taste

Mix sour cream and mayonnaise together, then mix all other ingredients together.
Serve with croissants or rolls.

The snowfall in Echo Ridge was beautiful—gorgeous snow globe-like flakes floating through the air, dusting the pine trees and making the road through the canyon a slick mess. Liza Sorenson checked the dashboard clock. It said 8:30 a.m., so there was plenty of time to drive carefully out of the canyon and into the heart of Echo Ridge, park in front of Stellar Ads, and set up for her presentation at nine.

"Okay, deep breath," Liza commanded herself. "You've got this." She pumped her brakes as she descended, watching the road for signs of white-tailed deer. The last thing she wanted was to hit a deer on the way to work today. She'd prepared a great presentation on how to easily make over and upgrade websites with copy editing techniques for their new clients. Hopefully, it would amaze her boss enough that he would consider Liza for a promotion.

She tapped the steering wheel of her car with her index finger as she mentally rehearsed the points of her presentation again. The snow was falling steadily and the flakes were sticking to the hood of her blue Ford Fusion, making it look like a speckled Easter egg.

If only they called snow days for work. Liza would stay home, curl up with her laptop, and write. But no, today was important and she would succeed at this job. She gripped the steering wheel tighter as she took the last stretch of road out of the canyon. The bare space on her left ring finger no longer taunted her, but there was still a painful twinge in her heart if she allowed her thoughts to go there.

Instead, she took a moment to appreciate her surroundings. There was a beautiful white two-story house with green shutters that she always admired on her way to work. The guy who lived there was technically her neighbor, but she didn't really know him, although she'd heard rumors that he was a bit of a bad boy. The white fence surrounding the acre of property had an inch of snow balancing along the rails. Everything was dressed in white this morning—the bushes, the trees, the mailbox, the white pickup in the driveway dusted with snow and—

"Noodles!" she screamed as she tried to dodge the

pickup backing out of the driveway. She swerved to the right, slamming on her brakes, but the tires had no grip on the ice. The car slid into the side of the pickup with a sickening crunch. Airbags bloomed around Liza's body, and then everything was quiet.

Liza groaned and rubbed the back of her neck, pushing the airbag out of the way. "No! This did not just happen. No!" Her body was stiff and tense, and she reminded herself to breathe. She turned her car off and was fumbling for the door handle when the door opened.

"Are you okay?" a man asked as he crouched down and pushed the airbag out of the way. "Did you hit your head?" He moved aside a lock of her hair, and their eyes met.

Liza stared at him. His eyes were framed with thick lashes, and the scruff on his cheeks made him appear rugged. He wore a gray wool coat with the collar turned up. What had he asked her?

He cocked his head, studying her with those arresting green eyes. "Are you okay?"

Wait. What was happening? She'd been in a wreck, and now she was checking out the guy who had totaled her car. He had asked her if she was okay. She shook her head and closed her eyes, groaning at the stiffness in her body. "No, I'm not all right!"

"Here, let me help you. Where are you hurt?" He

reached out his hand—his large, strong hand—and helped her from the car.

She stood blinking as the snowflakes fell on her lashes. "I don't think I'm hurt. Just my neck feels tight. You pulled out in front of me! I couldn't stop, and then the ice—everything is frozen!"

"I know. I'm sorry. I didn't get all the ice scraped off my windows, and I didn't see you. Are you sure you're not hurt?" He spoke with a musical cadence to his voice, and Liza felt herself leaning towards the low rumble.

This man had wrecked her car. She took a few steps forward to inspect the damage, almost wishing she could cover her eyes so she wouldn't have to see. The headlight on her passenger side was completely smashed and her fender had some serious dents, but it wasn't as bad as she thought—except when she stepped closer and saw that the smashed part of the car had tilted the tire at a weird angle.

"What am I going to do?" Liza turned toward the snowy road. "The cops won't get here for at least twenty minutes, and then it'll take them an hour to cite the accident. I'll miss my presentation!"

The man flinched. "Did you call the cops already?"

"No, I just need to find my phone. Or you can call them." Liza groaned again. "He's gonna fire me." How could this be happening? Just a few minutes ago, she'd been dreaming about getting promoted, and now her quick-to-fire boss would be waiting on her. Rick loved to threaten people with their jobs, and she'd seen enough people get fired to always walk on his right side.

"I'm not going to let you get fired. This is my mess, and I'll clean it up." He pulled his bottom lip between his teeth and then nodded. "I have an idea. You take my pickup to work; I'll get your car into the shop today and get it fixed up. Don't worry about cops and the insurance. I'll take care of everything."

"But—" Liza protested.

"But nothing. Let me handle it. Go to your meeting and I'll see you after work."

"But what if you're some kind of criminal? And this is just your method of stealing cars?" Liza could hear the hysteria in her voice, but she didn't know how to calm down. This guy had wrecked her car, and now she was thinking about walking away from the accident and leaving him with her vehicle?

He smiled, and Liza felt her knees go weak. She leaned against the car. Gosh, he was handsome, and was that a dimple? *Be strong, Liza!* She couldn't just walk away from an accident. Isn't that what everyone said? Never leave the scene of the accident without calling the police. But her job was on the line. And this handsome stranger was offering to fix her car and let her drive his pickup to work.

She looked over at the white Ford pickup. Well, at

least he had good taste. Her family was a Ford family. She sighed and took a closer look. The tires were brand-new and well-equipped for driving in Echo Ridge Canyon.

"My name is Jaime Maldonado. Here's my card with my number. Text me, and I'll update you on your car. You obviously know where I live, and no offense, but my pickup is a lot nicer than your car." He handed her the black electronic key fob. "Take it and be safe."

"I'm Liza Sorenson." She tucked the card in her pocket and curled her fingers around the key fob.

"It's nice to meet you, Liza, but I'm sorry we had to meet in this way," Jaime said.

She lifted her head, meeting his eyes. "Okay. I'm trusting you and I don't know why, but I guess it's because I don't have another option. I need this job."

Jaime pointed behind her. "I'm just going to jump in your car and back it up a little bit. No sense putting more scratches on my pickup."

Liza was going to reply with some sarcastic remark about him only caring about his pickup when she turned and saw the crumpled front end of her car. She shrugged. It was no use. She would think about it later. After her presentation. After she'd applied for the new position that her boss had been hinting about. She grabbed her bag and lunch sack out of the car, noticing that the stiffness in her neck had subsided. Hopefully, she could make it through the day.

She trudged through the snow and hopped into the heated leather seats of the pickup. The engine started up with the push of a button, and she searched for the defrost for a moment, then flipped it to high. She admired the display screen, which was larger than the one in her car. She changed the music from the local rock station to her favorite Christian music station and gripped the steering wheel. The leather was warm—the heated steering wheel was definitely a plus. After half a minute, she eased carefully out onto the highway and put the pickup into drive. Jaime waved to her as she drove away. She couldn't remember his last name. For a second, she questioned her sanity again. Maybe she'd hit her head in the accident. The responsible Liza would never leave her car broken down in some guy's driveway.

Wait, his business card would have a name on it. She fished it out of her pocket when she stopped at a red light. The card was printed in gray with black and white lettering. The design was simple, yet sleek and stylish. *Jaime Maldonado of Ratchet Revisions.* Underneath his name in script was printed, *Translation and editing services for your online business.*

She knew his name and his business now. She also knew that he was ruggedly handsome. No, he was gorgeous—more beautiful than should be humanly possible. He drove the nicest pickup she'd ever seen, and even though he'd wrecked her car, she would be seeing him again later that day. She told herself that the flutter in her stomach was because she was nervous about being late for her presentation. It didn't have anything to do with his caramel-colored skin, black hair, and green eyes.

Continue reading *HER GUY NEXT DOOR FAKE FIANCE* available in print, ebook, and audio. Find out more information at

www.rachellechristensen.com

If you enjoyed this Echo Ridge Romance from Rachelle J. Christensen, you may also enjoy her other sweet romance series, Burke Billionaire Romance. Enjoy this sneak peek of book #1 *Hawaiian Masquerade*.

Keep reading for a sneak peek of #1 Burke Billionaire Romance

Hawaiian Masquerade

CHAPTER ONE

Lexi stared at the tube of cadmium red oil paint hanging from the shelf, remembering how expensive that color had seemed in college. She grabbed it and ten additional tubes in a rainbow of colors—the first step on a new path in life. The squeaking wheel of the shopping cart gave voice to the trepidation crawling up her spine, telling her she was nuts for leaving behind a life that most people claimed they wanted. But Lexi knew something that most people didn't: millions and millions of dollars did not create a wellspring of happiness. Cold hard cash was, in fact, cold and hard.

Kauai was not cold. The brilliant sunshine and perfumed air was freely available to everyone on the island. Roadways were drenched in color from vibrant greens to bright pinks and accented with the red dirt Kauai was known for. Lexi studied the brushes available and chose a long-handled round brush that would help her recreate the beautiful landscapes of the island. Now if she could find a few canvases, she would be ready to paint on the beach outside her home. She turned down another aisle and saw a display of white rectangles and squares. They were wrapped in plastic, but Lexi ran her finger along the edges; the rough feel of a blank canvas and the possibility it represented brought back pleasant memories.

A toddler's shrill cry snapped her out of her musings. She steered her cart around a stack of twelve-by-eighteen-inch canvases and found the source. The little girl couldn't have been more than two years old, tiny with fine black hair pulled back in pigtails. Her red hibiscus-print dress set off dark caramel skin, and even as her wail intensified, Lexi found herself admiring the pretty Polynesian girl.

That's when she noticed that the toddler was alone. Lexi glanced around, but this area of the store was empty. She stepped forward carefully and crouched in front of the girl. "Sweetie, are you lost?"

As soon as the words left her mouth, the little girl held out her arms and reached for Lexi. She sniffled, melting Lexi's heart as she carefully picked up the child. She looked down the aisle, hoping to see the little girl's mother, but at the same time nervous that the mother would think her daughter was being kidnapped. Lexi patted the girl's back, and she snuggled closer. Swallowing against the sudden lump in her throat, Lexi focused on the task at hand.

Turning slowly to scan the store again, she saw a man with dark hair, a chiseled jawline, and a worried crease in his forehead. He was tall with golden-brown skin and wore a green tank top that showed off his finely sculpted biceps. Something shifted in Lexi's heart. It thumped hard twice, and blood rose to her cheeks. The man stared back at her, his face open, revealing an arc of emotions as he took in the sight of the little girl and Lexi—wonder, admiration, curiosity, and something else she couldn't define.

She stepped forward, eyebrows raised in question. "Is she yours?"

His dark hair was spiked on top and close-shaven on the sides. He sported a bit of scruff that Lexi could only describe as sexy. One side of his mouth lifted, and he shook his head. "No, is she lost?"

"Yes, she was crying right over here, and I've stayed put for a minute hoping her mom would show up looking for her."

He turned around in a slow circle, repeating the search Lexi had undertaken moments before, having a better view over the shelves because he was taller. Oh, so tall and sculpted. "I can help you find her parents. This store isn't that big. Maybe they haven't missed her yet."

Lexi's brow furrowed in protest as she struggled to rein in her emotions. It had been at least three minutes since she'd heard the toddler's cries, and five minutes was like an eternity in a child's world—surely it would feel just as long for a frantic parent searching for her child. She gently patted the girl's back. "It's okay, sweetie, I know what it feels like to be lost," she murmured. Then she realized that the man was standing close enough to hear her. She straightened, cleared her throat, and spoke louder. "We'll help you."

The man pointed to the other side of the store. "I'll go this way, you go that way?"

"That's a good idea." Lexi smiled, and her stomach flipped when the man returned her smile. The little girl moved her head, quiet and warm in Lexi's arms.

The man walked quickly across the store, and Lexi went in the other direction. There was only one other shopper, an old man with a handful of charcoal and sketch pads. Lexi smiled at him, and he winked at her and the little girl. "Beautiful kaikamahine."

Lexi nodded, appreciating the melodic Hawaiian language. The man saw them as mother and daughter, which was a stretch considering Lexi's fair skin, blond hair, and green eyes. She held the child close. They were two lost souls trying to find something to keep them safe. Lexi was certain she'd find the little girl's mother, but what could Lexi find that would fill the need in her heart?

"Here she is," someone said from behind Lexi. She turned around and saw that the dark-haired man was leading a Polynesian woman with long dark hair toward her. "Safe and sound."

"Keilani! Oh, baby," the woman said. "I'm so glad you're okay."

The little girl immediately sat up and reached her arms out. She cried for a few seconds, clinging to her mother, clutching her light cotton shirt.

"Mahalo. Oh, thank you so much for finding my baby," the woman gushed.

"She's a sweetheart," Lexi said. "She wanted me to hold her, and that seemed to help while we looked for you."

"One minute she was there, and then she was gone. You know how kids are." The woman patted her daughter's back. "Keilani, say thank you to the beautiful lady who found you," the woman said, looking down at her daughter with a smile.

The toddler looked at Lexi and held her hand out, moving it back and forth. Then she giggled and blew Lexi a kiss.

Lexi pretended to catch the kiss in the air and patted her cheek. "Thank you, Keilani. Have fun shopping."

She waved at the little girl, then let her hand drop to her side. That's when she noticed the man who had helped her standing quietly next to the end cap of paintbrushes on aisle seven. "You really get the credit for finding her," Lexi said. "Thanks for hunting down the lost mother."

He grinned. "Glad to help out a tourist when I can."

"But I'm not a tourist," Lexi replied. "I just moved here."

One eyebrow lifted, and Lexi noticed a shift in his brown eyes, as if he were seeing her for the first time. He held out his hand. "That's great news. Aloha, and welcome to Kauai. I'm Derek Mitchell."

They shook hands, and a sensation like warm, salty

spray went up her arm. When they broke contact, she immediately craved his touch again. What was happening to her? The first hot guy to shake her hand had her thinking of moonlight walks on the beach and kisses in the sand. She decided that she was smitten with the *idea* of this Hawaiian guy. She needed a can of chocolate-covered macadamia nuts and a long bath, not a man. Still, she smiled broadly and returned the introduction. "I'm Lexi Burke, no longer from Chicago."

Derek wrinkled his nose. "Man, that place is cold. Good choice coming here in March. The weather will only get better from now until October."

"I'm counting on it," Lexi replied.

"Are you an artist?" Derek asked, motioning to the growing stack of supplies in Lexi's cart, which she'd left in the middle of the aisle.

"I wish." Lexi laughed as she grabbed the handle. "Maybe in a different lifetime—or maybe now. I love art, and I need to refocus some of my energy. Drawing and painting used to be a passion of mine, before the nine-to-five killed it."

Derek nodded. "I get that. The good thing about this place is it unwinds all that tension, and creativity leaks out from everywhere." He tipped his head to the side. "Since you're new, I'll let you in on a secret. Drive over to Hanapepe tomorrow—Friday night is the local art night—and you'll see what I mean."

"Hmm, I may just do that." Lexi gave Derek her canned response to every invite from the male species. And then she realized that he was being friendly. Maybe she could go . . . but then she might run into him, and he was too good-looking with that bronzed skin and his relaxed stance that seemed to say, *I don't have any idea what my looks do to your pulse rate.* Yep. Derek was on her list of things not to encounter in Kauai. Her fingertips drummed along the plastic-wrapped handle of her shopping cart, trying to keep up with her racing heart. It was time to make a quick exit. "Thanks again for your help. Maybe I'll see you around the island sometime."

"Good luck with the painting." Derek lifted one hand and let it fall. He had a stack of frames tucked under his other arm.

After checking out and packing the supplies into her Jeep, Lexie wished she hadn't been so skittish around Derek and missed the opportunity to reciprocate his interest in her new hobby. He'd spoken about creativity, and judging by the frames and his knowledge of the Hanapepe street fair, he was probably an artist himself. There she was, thinking about him again. Derek was just another piece of man candy Lexi didn't want to taste, even if he'd been kind and genuine at the store. She shouldn't be mean to him just because she carried a chip on her shoulder the size of the Sears Tower. She could give him the benefit of the doubt. Derek was quite possibly delicious on the inside, too.

Then again, so was the authentic Hawaiian shaved ice Lexi was going to pick up at Hee Fat General Store. Yes, ice covered in sugar sitting on top of a mountain of thick ice cream would definitely do the trick to keep Lexi's mind from wandering into dangerous territory.

Keep reading *Hawaiian Masquerade* available in print, ebook, and audio. For more information, visit

www.rachellechristensen.com

Photo by Erin Summerill

Rachelle writes mystery/suspense, clean romance, and women's fiction. She is the mother of a large family and she solves the case of the missing shoe on a daily basis. She enjoys raising chickens, laughing with her family, and traveling with her husband. She graduated cum laude from Utah State University with a degree in psychology and a minor in music.

Rachelle is the award-winning author of over twenty books, including *The Soldier's Bride (a Kindle Scout Selection)*, the Rone award winner for mystery, *River Whispers*, *Diamond Rings Are Deadly Things*, *Hawaiian Masquerade*, and *the Echo Ridge Romance series*. Her novella, "Silver Cascade Secrets," was included in the Rone Award–winning *Timeless Romance Anthology, Fall Collection*.

Join Rachelle's VIP mailing list to learn more about upcoming books and get your free book at www.rachellechristensen.com.

Thrills for the Heart

FOR A LIMITED TIME

Sign up for Rachelle's
VIP Mailing List
to get your *FREE* book.

★ ★ ★ ★ ★

Get started here:
www.rachellechristensen.com